TATER AND THE MYSTICAL BONEYARD

ROSE WHITE

Editor: Jade Branum

TATER AND THE MYSTICAL BONEYARD

iUniverse books may be ordered through booksellers or by contacting:

iUniverse
1663 Liberty Drive
Bloomington, IN 47403
www.iuniverse.com
1-800-Authors (1-800-288-4677)

ISBN: 978-1-5320-1181-8 (sc)
ISBN: 978-1-5320-1182-5 (e)

Library of Congress Control Number: 2017905884

Print information available on the last page.

iUniverse rev. date: 06/15/2017

For James
and our boy, Artie.
German Shepard/Great Dane Mix

CHAPTER ONE

The last of summer heat saturated Jenny Brown as she turned her bike off the main highway onto the dirt road. The landscape was heavy with overgrown trees, their branches looming toward the ground. Grass was growing everywhere. The sound of lawnmowers filled the air. Pines, sweet gums, and oaks dotted the country side. It was down south, not way down south but near the coast. The Carolina sun was hot and merciless in August.

Jennifer Antoinette Brown rode like the wind, her twelve year old lungs were strong and able to take the extreme heat and humidity of her world. She stood on the petals for balance as she took curves at full speed. A true athlete, Jenny could have been any any race, anywhere. Jenny was a fit, active girl. She had a deep tan and kept her shoulder length black hair tied back in a pony-tail most of the summer. Her mother encouraged her to dress simply and with modest taste. Jenny idolized her mother. Although Mom was dead, Jenny remembered how she dresses, how she fixed her hair and she wanted to be just like her. Jennifer carefully chose complimentary colors. Today, it was lavender shorts and a yellow top with a dark purple bathing suit underneath.

As she peddled, she noticed new things, like cleared woods, bull dozers, sand piles or any change. Her town was named after the first president and her neighborhood was once country, full of horses, cows and roosters. Now, people from all over were coming to build. Her daddy said, "People coming down here with pockets full of cash, running up the land prices and taking all the supervisor jobs."

Jennifer tried to get along with the new names and new faces, to her, north and south was just another boring thing learned in social studies and geography. At least, northern teachers called her Jennifer. Older southern women called her Jennifer Antoinette, and Jenny hated her middle name.

◠✐◡

She passed old Joe Lee's ugly house. It was the ugliest house she had ever seen. The white wooden shack with weeds growing where his long deceased wife's roses used to bloom. A pen was just to the right of the house. The hunting dogs lay almost lifeless in the late morning sun. Usually, Jenny did not dare look at them, for fear they might be too hot or thirsty, but today was different.

Joe Lee was known to take a drink or two and sound off with his shot gun at dusk. No one cared. The dogs looked out in the distance with a dull stare until they saw Jenny. They lifted their heads and perked their ears. Some mornings when she knew Joe Lee was gone, she would throw ice from the freezer into their near empty water buckets. She would empty all the ice trays and peddle fast before the ice would melt away. Dumping the ice in their water buckets, the dogs would lick the chunks of ice, grateful for the relief and short comfort they experienced.

Jenny had brought ice this morning. She reached into the baggie and tossed each cube into the buckets. Excited, the dogs scrambled to get an ice cube.

Feeling happy, Jenny reached down and grabbed a dandelion which had gone to seed.

Holding the stem and staring at the seeds, Jenny thought hard for the perfect wish. "If I had one wish in the whole world, I would grow up and help all the dogs without good homes." She inhaled deeply and blew. The seeds scattered in the air.

Next was the Moore house.

"Hey, Mrs. Moore, ninety eight degrees today!" yelled Jenny, never slowing her stride.

Ella More had a nice, brick home. She kept her yard as neat as her house which was perfect. She sat on the porch until noon. She would grin and wave at Jenny who waved back and pulled up to her porch.

"Whew, that's hot!" said Mrs. Moore.

"I am meeting my friend at the river to cool off," said Jenny.

"I saw you over there with those hunting dogs. Leave them be. Your daddy don't need no more trouble. With your Momma dying in that horrible accident, he can't afford a thing to happen to you."

"I know, Ms. Morris, but I feel sorry for those dogs. They have no water."

"He a mean man, that Joe Lee." said Ms. Morris.

Changing the subject, Ms. Morris smiled and said, "You know. I think I saw the little Porter girl ghost last night. I looked out my bedroom window and heard a faint cry. She come close to my yard from the woods. All dressed in white, pale, walking in circles, like she looking for something."

Chills went down Jenny's spine. She looked up at the roof that was higher than the pines. It was as if the Porter house loomed over the whole town. In it's heyday, the massive Porter Mansion was built on a hill overlooking the Tar River. The Porter family owned most of the farm land in Beaufort County. Abandoned for a hundred years, the family lost their lives in a fire that only destroyed the house in part. The house had multiple rooms and entrances. Enough remained to still have a dominating presence. Jenny was afraid of the house and of the rumored ghost girl who was said to haunt the woods at night.

"I got to go, Ms. Morris! She pushed down on the peddle and started off.

"You be careful in that water. Your daddy and sister need you!" yelled Ms. Morris as Jenny peddled away.

At the end of the road was the metal fence with the gate open. In the water right under the pier was Daniel, Jenny's best friend since third grade. He was already in the river. There were two plastic donut floats on the pier. It was overcast but Jenny had brought some sun lotion, just in case. She laid down her bike and jumped in!

"I am so hot!" yelled Jenny at her friend.

"It's cold in here!" Daniel cupped his hands around his mouth to make his voice louder. He was a small framed boy with light hair about as tall as Jenny.

A fence would go up with a big private property sign above a gate. As for now, Jenny and Daniel hid the floats on the land in some bushes. It had been their private pool for the last three years, but they both knew it was their last summer.

"Water wars!" yelled Daniel. He took his hand and held it flat with the fingers tightly together. He then skimmed his hand over the water's surface causing a splash in Jenny's face.

"You're on." She sprayed his face and they kept on until they both gasped for air.

"Look, fart bubbles!" laughed Daniel. A few bubbles came to the surface.

"Gross out. That is so not cool." said Jenny, as she gently maneuvered around back of him. He did not see the 'wedgey' coming. She dove under and grabbed his shorts and pulled hard.

Jenny and Daniel both had three things in common. They were twelve and neither one had a mother to over protect them. Both fathers were overworked and could not keep an eye on their choice of activities so they provided safety for each other. Throw backs, into another time, they were out on their own. No soccer moms for them.

They chilled a bit and watched the construction on the house in front of them.

"The house beside ours is almost finished. It is so huge and so fancy." said Jenny.

"Yeah, they are taking all the fun places. You know, the clay hills over by the quarry?"

"Yeah."

"Chain link fence. Future home of Luxury Condos, a Place for You."

"I have seen that sign. This is the last place on the river not taken." commented Jenny.

Jenny and Daniel both looked east. They stared at the house in the distance. It's brick chimney could be barely seen above the woods since it was overgrown with trees. There was a road that led there but it was covered with grass and weeds just like the old, weather scarred plantation house that overlooked the river. The path was clear enough for all the kids who went to explore the Porter mansion.

But Jenny and Daniel stayed off the road and on the path to the river. They treaded water and looked around.

"Are they taking the Porter house?" Daniel asked.

"I don't know. But I wish they would!" said Jenny.

They both had heard the legend of the Porter mansion. There were many stories about the old house, some true and some pure fiction. It was haunted, they said. Escapees from the prison in the next town often hid out there. All the grown ups say that kids that go there never come back. Each generation added to the lore of the old house, making it more alluring. In other words, the more stories, the more kids wanted to go explore it, but Jenny already had.

"Let's go up there." said Daniel.

'Why is everyone is talking about that old house today?' thought Jenny. She shook her head, NO, and went under the water holding her nose.

Jennifer had been to the house when she was only four. Her babysitter, Christina Lovell was a teenager, barely sixteen, who met her boyfriend up at the mansion while she was keeping Jennifer for her parents, George and Sandra Brown. Jenny was so young. She remembered meeting a little girl in the house. She was blonde and had on a white gown. Christina and her boyfriend had set up a tent. They planned to spend the night with Jenny.

Jenny did not hear Christina call her. The little blonde girl wanted her to go deep in the woods. Jenny followed her.

"I want my dolly." said the blonde girl.

"Dolly…" said Jenny back. The girl vanished. Jennifer ran after her. Christina and her boyfriend did not notice.

Jennifer remembered being lost in the woods and crying. A fireman found her.

Later, Jennifer overheard her parents talking about Christina. She learned that Christina and her boyfriend had gone to get help. When the fire department started to form a search party, Christina collapsed and had to be hospitalized for third degree burns. It was a mystery. She had smoke in her lungs. But there had been no fire. The house remained empty and desolate and there were no forest fires or even any fires in all of Beaufort County. Jenny was unharmed.

Jennifer and Daniel swirled in their round floats for a few minutes.

"I don't want to go anywhere but the river. I brought us some drinks." said Jenny.

Daniel lifted himself out of the water on the pier. He was a small boy for his age but was agile and strong. He lifted his weight up easily with two hands, swung his leg over and reached for a can of soda. He tossed one to Jenny.

"Where's Mary Beth? She any better?" asked Daniel.

"No, the same. She is watching the cartoon channel and will be all day. The doctor said there was nothing wrong with her legs, she has something wrong with her brain. I don't know." Jenny answered.

Her mother and sister were in a car accident last fall, when the leaves had turned yellow and the coolness of night had set in. Sandra, Jenny's mother had died on the scene but Mary Beth had survived.

After several attempts at making the perfect belly flop dive, both were content to lay on their donuts and discuss their options in the fall.

"I have Mrs. Mann for math next year." said Daniel with a worried tone.

"Yeah, so do I. I hear she is very strict, sends two or three kids to the 'chill out' room every day. I have Mrs. Motto for English and Mrs. Berney for social studies." commented Jenny.

"Oh man. You know what I heard about Mrs. Berney?"

"What, not the mouth wash rumor?" asked Jenny carefully.

"I swear it's true. She constantly brushes her teeth and swallows the mouthwash for the alcohol! I saw her."

"I will believe it when I see it." said Jenny. Nothing was more delightful than gossiping about their past and future teachers. It seemed to level the playing field a little. They had no choice about who they had, so a little gossip was fair. A beep came from the dock.

"Oh, crap. That's my dad." Daniel swam over to the pier.

"I wish I had my own cell phone. Mary Beth and I have to share." said Jenny.

"It's his way of keeping a leash on me." Daniel held it up and showed her the phone.

"He has texted me a reminder to mow the grass or I am in deep trouble."

Jenny had enough sun and climbed on the pier with Daniel. They agreed to change clothes and meet up later after supper. Jenny had to do the cooking for her father and sister.

Daniel froze on the pier and said "Oh crap."

Jenny lifted herself out of the water and saw Zeb Lee, Joe Lee's nephew messing with Daniel's bike on the small beach. He had kicked it over in the water and had a hand full of river sand. He looked over at Jenny's bike. Zeb was nearly five foot nine and weighed at least two hundred pounds. He had dark wavy hair and pimples. Kids called him the Walking Zit but never to his face.

"I like the girl's bike better. You been messin' with my uncle's dogs Jennifer Antwoinette Brown."

"Leave our bikes alone." Daniel said. He approached the large boy with confidence but Zeb pushed him with both hands and Daniel fell back in the water. Zeb was not bright. He was strong, very strong and Jenny knew it.

"I was just being nice. Why don't you go home and give them some water. That would be very nice Zeb." Jenny spoke to him as if he were a toddler.

"No, I rather take your bike. Your little boyfriend ain't gonna stop me." He laughed a slow, dumb laugh looking at Daniel who was clutching a piece of driftwood which was jagged at one end. It was the size of a log six inches in diameter.

"Not if I can help it." Daniel said. He watched Jenny go around the back of Zeb with a donut float. She acted as if she were playing a game of charades. Lifted the float she showed Daniel she would put it over Zeb's head and then she looked at the driftwood piece and made a jabbing motion.

"But you can't take her bike. Take mine." Daniel pulled up the driftwood and pointed at his bike. "I will even get it for you."

"It is all wet." laughed Zeb.

With a the cunning of a hunter springing a trap, Jenny put the donut over his head and yanked back. Daniel rammed the driftwood in the stomach. All three fell on the beach. Daniel punched his face until he saw Zeb was about to cry.

"I'm telling." Zeb cried. He had some scratches on his stomach but other wise all three were alright.

"I'm telling." Zeb was wailing now. He walked to the road repeating the empty threat over and over.

"It is so sad. I used to play with him in first grade." Jenny said. "He needs to have foster parents or something."

"His uncle made him a bully, my dad says. You know he will forget all about this the first time someone offers him food." Daniel replied.

"I know," said Jenny, "Mrs. Drummond used to keep candy bars in her desk just for Zeb. He went away for a while and came back. I know he will be in some of our classes."

Hiding the floats under a bush with a few bricks to weigh them down and washing the mud off his bike, Daniel hollered, "Bye."

Jenny already had her bike in gear and was tossing gravel and dirt as she built up speed.

Jenny peddled the mile to her home. The neighborhood was under siege, with bulldozers and the sound of construction workers. Jenny's house was right beside prime development land. Her home was a modest three bedroom white brick ranch. There were identical houses up and down the road. A contractor had built them just alike. That was back in 1962. The people of that time wanted houses to be alike, even and straight. But as their children grew up, the houses began to change so each had become unique over time. Each house was a little different in color or additions. Jenny was a baby when her mother and father moved into their home. They were right beside the road. Across the road were woods, untouched for years. Wildlife was plentiful. Jenny once saw a bear in her back yard.

In those very woods, another house, twice the size of Jenny's modest home, was almost completed. The owners were from out west. The new houses would be called Forest Lawn Estates. Jenny's block was full of older homes and trailers filled with the previous generation of native Washington residents. Her dad had lived in Washington since birth.

Jenny jumped off her bike and headed in. Mary Beth was watching cartoons in her wheelchair. Mary was a pretty girl who looked like a smaller version of her sister. Her face was blank as she stared at the television. The living room was decorated with simple but worn furniture. It was a neat house. Jennifer kept it that way.

There was one bedroom which had remained closed and two small bedrooms were on the right. When Sandra Brown died, George put his wife's possessions in the closed room. It became a memorial for the girls' mother and anytime they wanted to be near her the could go in and sit on the bed, look at her dresses, look at little keepsakes in her jewelry box. But everyone knew to put things back just as they found them in respect for their mother. The girls stayed in the two rooms and her father slept on the couch. Jenny undressed as she headed for the bathroom, picking up the clothes as she stripped.

"Mary Beth, did you wash the dishes? It is my night to cook." asked Jenny. Her dad walked in the back door.

Mary Beth did not answer and only laughed at Sponge Bob Square Pants. Jenny was irritated by her sister sloughing off chores but would defend her like a tiger protecting her cubs if someone else would say anything negative to Mary Beth.

Mary Beth rolled up to the sink and her father and sister helped her stand at the sink. Her therapist encouraged such use of her legs. Mary Beth did not avoid helping Jenny while her father was in the house. He was very strict and disliked it when Jenny had to do all the work.

George Brown was a small man in stature. He had a dark tan from being outside all day. He wore a baseball hat most of the time and had a mustache and short beard.

"Girls, I have to tell you something. There is a trucking job that will pay a lot more money than the quarry but I will have to be away from home."

"How long?" asked Mary Beth.

"About two weeks at a time, maybe a month." answered George.

"I can take care of things." volunteered Jenny.

"No, you are too young." George hesitated. "You know I have been seeing Ms. Vivian socially for three months now.

"Yes, we know." answered Jenny. She began getting a knot in her stomach. Jenny did not like Ms. Vivian. Ms. Vivian had a daughter her age named Linda Kaye who was the biggest snob in the whole school. Like a calico cat, Linda Kaye had several colors of hair. In pony tails, she kept blonde hair on the right side off her head, brown hair on the left with a purple streak on the blonde side. She wore the best of clothes. With her cell phone in hand, Linda Kaye ruled the school by constantly talking with the most popular kids of West Beaufort Middle school. She roamed the halls with a pack of girls around her, more than willing to do her bidding, just to be near Linda Kay. It made Jenny shutter to think about her. They both would be in seventh grade this year. Mary Beth was going to be in sixth.

"We have decided to pool our money, she and her daughter are moving in next week. I have decided to take the job." George stopped helping the girls and put his hands on his hips for their reaction.

"No way, dad. I would rather move in with Aunt Mamie.! We talked about that right after Mom died." Jenny pleaded.

"Aunt Mamie is your Mom's older sister and we love her. But she is not quite right in the head. She imagines having children who do not exist. At last count there were thirty cats in her house before the law had to come take them out."

"But Dad, Ms Vivian does not like us." countered Jenny.

"She's mean." added Mary Beth.

"If I can make a go at this trucking deal for a year, it is possible for me to look around in other towns while I am working. Girls, the quarry is killing me. I am not a young man anymore. I have to find something for the long haul. Something that I can be building a future for you both. This neighborhood is full of quarry widows. Men either move on or die. I need to move on while I am able to learn something new."

"What is a quarry?" asked Mary Beth.

"We make little rocks out of big rocks. For drive ways." George answered.

Jenny argued but her Dad's mind was made up. She bolted out the back door with the scraps from supper. She could not shake off the thought of Linda Kaye coming into her home. It was impossible.

"Jenny!" yelled George. She stopped and turned to look at her father. "You be careful around that old man and his dog."

"Tater is friendly, Dad, and the old man is never at home." yelled Jenny back.

"All right, it is almost dark. Come right back, I mean it." said her father sternly.

Tater was a young and clumsy Great Dane that lived about three houses down from Jenny's house. The dog was the size of a small pony. Daniel and Jenny discovered her last year while skateboarding. It was what felt like a life time ago, but it was just a year, when Jenny's mother was alive.

"Do you hear something?" asked Daniel and they practiced mounting their skateboards with one foot. Jenny stopped. She looked down at the road and listened.

"Shh!" she motioned Daniel to stop his board. It was a whine and a whimper. They picked up their skateboards and followed the sound.

Old man Quinn's yard was full of junk. He had the most land in her neighborhood but it was overgrown with sapling trees, grass and thistles. He was a collector. Rows of old air condition units were followed by eight push movers lying like dead soldiers on a battle field. There were mounds of wire and springs. Later, while curiously exploring his yard, Jenny would open a storage bin and find hundreds of plastic toys from Happy Meals. Following the sound, Jenny and Daniel saw the most beautiful dog on a long chain. It was caught around a tree and the dog could barely move much less get to the water bucket which was almost empty.

"We have to help it." said Jenny.

"What if it bites? I mean that is one big dog." retorted Daniel. They stared at the dog for a few more minutes. The dog began barking and became excited by their presence.

"Dad showed me how to approach a dog. You do not act afraid of it. Do not move a whole lot. Put your hand out so it can sniff you. If the dog growls and stiffens, then it will bite. If it wags its' tail, you can pet it."

"You first, then." said Daniel.

Jenny now had to put her advice to practice. She stopped about midway.

"Maybe we should call the Humane Society." said Daniel.

"They will put the dog in the pound." said Jenny.

"I think the dog is friendly." Jenny took a deep breath and moved toward the dog. It sniffed Jenny's hand and wagged it's whole body with a friendly demeanor which demanded play. Jenny gently petted the dog. It jumped around and crouched invited Jenny and Daniel to play.

"Now, don't get upset. I am going to unleash you."

The dog panted and tried to jump. Jenny reached it and found the latch on the chain. She unleashed the dog which pounded for Daniel.

"Oh no!" Daniel dropped his skateboard and started to run when a hundred pounds of Great Dane overtook him. Daniel rolled on his back and raised his hands to protect his face from the massive beast but found out the dog was not a fighter but a lover. The dog began licking Daniel's face.

"Gross!" Daniel stood up and said, "Down, good dog, down."

Jenny untangled the chain.

"I guess we should chain her back up."

"How do you know it is a girl?" asked Daniel, now petting the large excited dog. The dog rolled on her back exposing her belly.

Jenny petted her belly and said, "look for yourself." Daniel turned red.

"Find a water hose!" Jenny ordered.

"What if the old man comes home? We can get into trouble being back here." said Daniel. "My dad has me on probation any ways. One more screw up and I loose all my privileges."

"I see a hose." Jenny ignored Daniel's fear of getting caught and took the bucket over to the hose, turned it on and began filling it up the bucket.

"We just can't leave her without water." said Jenny. "Hurry up."

Daniel led the dog back to the chain and clipped it on the collar.

"At least she has shade." Jenny put the water bucket just at the dog's reach, so it could not be knocked over by the dog's frantic movements. The dog lapped it up.

Jenny knew her mother, Sandra cared deeply for her two girls. They were her world. She had to work but would always put her girls before her work. The dental office was, at least, ten until five and she had every Friday off. Sandra went to every parent teacher conference and worked at being a super mom on the weekends. She was a sweet, soft spoken, woman. She loved working with the girl scout troops and sold cookies every year at the local grocery store.

With a soft but strong look about her, Sandra told Jenny it was wrong of her to go on Mr. Quinn's land without his permission. Jenny pleaded about the dog's living conditions.

"We just can't let it die." said Jenny with tears welling up in her eyes. Her mother smiled.

"Let's try some diplomacy. If it does not work, we need to call the humane society. You cannot keep trespassing on his land." said Sandra.

Later, Sandra stood with a plate full of brownies wrapped in cellophane at Mr. Quinn's door. Jenny hid behind her peering at the fat, old man opening the door. He wore a blue shirt tucked into his pants.

"Yes?" he asked.

"Mr. Quinn. How are you?" asked Mrs. Brown. My name is Sandra and I live a few houses down. My daughter, Jenny, has become attached to your dog. She has been feeding it scraps and I want to apologize for her being so forward."

"That's all right. Come in. Come in." said Mr. Quinn. He was relieved. Most people were trying to buy "his stuff" as he called it. Sandra held out the brownies and offered condolences on Mrs. Quinn who had died the previous year. After some coaxing and some promises that Jenny would not mess with "his stuff", Mr. Quinn said it was all right for Jenny to feed and water the dog.

"Her name is Tater." said Mr. Quinn scratching head. "She is a Great Dane with papers. A man owed me a lot of money for some car parts and he wouldn't pay. He didn't think that I would take his dog when he offered it for payment, but I did. A bird in the hand is better than two in the bush."

"Why is her name 'Tater'?" asked Jenny.

"She has a name as long as my arm on those dog papers, but I gave her fried tater tots and she loved them. So I called her 'Tater'? It fits."

So, Jenny developed a routine of checking in on the dog at dusk and giving it dog-biscuits and water. She saved her allowance and bought she proper dry food which she put on the old man's back porch. Sometimes, she would mix it with table scraps. The only time she did not visit Tater was the week after her mother's death.

CHAPTER TWO

"You are not going to believe this!" Jenny called Daniel on her cell while walking to Tater's house.

"Linda Kaye is moving into my house! I am in shock!"

"Oh, man. Your house is going to become the party house. Snap. Linda is good looking!" said Daniel with youthful optimism.

"I can't stand to look at her and her toadies. How am I going to live with her?" countered Jenny. She closed up the phone and stuffed it in her jean's pocket. Tater was raring up. She barked and paced back and forth. The dog brayed as Great Danes do. The creature almost sounded like a horse. Jenny petted her and cried a little. Tater looked at Jenny with understanding eyes and cocked her head when Jenny spoke.

"It's not fair, Tater. How can my Dad do this to us without even asking? Linda Kaye's mother is so scary!"

The dog ate it's treats and sat down and looked as if to hear every word. Jenny told the dog of her fears of starting seventh grade and having Linda Kaye in her house, day and night. At dusk, Jenny walked home as her father had told her to do.

Just like the mysterious Porter House, Ms. Vivian was part of the landscape and feared by most children. She worked at a Stop and Go. From a kid's perspective, the thirty five year old woman was huge and scary. She wore clothing from the local K-Mart and preferred pinks and purples with sequins. Her pants were often extra-large stretch pants. She wore studded flip flops and bedroom shoes behind the counter at work. When she waited on customers she always made eye contact. It was as if she could see right through anyone. She stared outward with large eyes made to seem even larger with the purple eye make-up. Her long golden tinted red hair pulled up in a style fit for a ball. It made her seem even taller.

She always remained calm and through an icy glare, she stopped misbehavior before it started.

Jenny knew the story of Mike Wainright, boy who challenged Ms. Vivian's authority one late Thursday afternoon. The story grew with time, more funny and more scary with each telling.

Mike was twelve years old, a tall boy for his age. He had red hair and spiked it up with gel. All of his teachers spent hours on the phone with his parents who did not take Mike's antics as concerned guardians but as the architects of a cruel bully. He had his come-uppance the day he decided he would play a trick on Ms. Vivian. He walked through the convenience store with his pants hanging down, a large T-shirt went down to his knees. He stuffed a couple of candy bars in his pants when Ms. Vivian was ringing up another customer. He selected a third candy bar and nodded to this audience on the other side of the store glass. His friends gathered in a group with one boy who had his nose planted against the glass. He relayed Mike's actions like a sports caster covering a ball game.

"He's going up to the counter. She's giving him the look. The boy laughed, "He's doing it!" They all laughed. Mike slapped the candy bar on the register and emptied out his pocket. He had taken a hundred pennies from his sister's piggy bank.

"Lift your shirt." Ms. Vivian ordered.

"What? No, lady, are you weird or what?" He laughed.

Ms. Vivian reached out with a large hand, painted fingernails and the clatter of her many bracelets and rings and pulled his shirt collar over his head enough to expose the candy bars. Mike pulled away. Ms. Vivian kept a cup of popcorn oil and a hand gun behind the counter to foil any one leaving the store without paying. She tossed some of the oil on the floor and slowly walked around the counter. Mike tried to run but he slipped on the oil. He struggled and landed flat on his face. The large hand grabbed his pants, pulling them up. Mike's feet were still slipping and sliding on the floor. He made one last attempt to run but when he hit the glass and fell back onto the popcorn oil. His friends had ran away. So the rest of the story is just imagined or conjecture.

Some say Mike was spanked over Ms. Vivian's knee like a misbehaved toddler, others say she stripped him to his underwear, making him walk home in his 'tighty whities' and other say he was arrested. One boy said she grabbed them by his hair and slapped him silly, telling him to go get out, stay out and to wear his pants right. Being disrespectful to Ms. Vivian could scar a child for life, or at least, that is the thinking of any young shoplifters that may have the notion of stealing in Ms. Vivian's store. Jenny heard from a teacher that Mike's parents did speak to Ms Vivian but she never moved from her stool behind the counter, never smiled and she said very little. No one really knew for sure, but Mike changed from a problem to a model student in one day. His mother began picking him up from school early. He did not want to pass Ms. Vivian, not even with his friends.

"He goes to a counselor now. What did your Mom do to him?" asked Jennifer while Linda Kaye was standing behind her in the lunch line.

"She just has a way of telling you what you need to do and how you need to be."

"Hope she never tells me."

"Easy, pay for your candy."

On the way home from school Jenny and her father made a detour to the Stop and Go. Jenny went in for a candy bar. George Brown pulled something from the back seat of the car and walked into the mini-mart and laid a large bouquet of flowers on the counter. George had known Ms. Vivian since she was a girl and he admired her.

"I read that your husband died and you have one daughter. I am sorry, I never sent a card or flowers when he died. I know Joe was a lumber man, hard working. I lost my wife a few months ago. I have two girls." He looked at his shoes. "I am babbling." She cracked a small smile that one might have detected with binoculars. Not waiting to be asked, Ms. Vivian said, "Saturday night. Seven o'clock." Her large hands scooped up the flowers and put them in a vase from aisle three.

"That will be ten dollars for the vase." George pulled out a bill, laid it on the counter and tipped his hat to her as he left the store.

Jenny gasped and hid behind the candy isle.

CHAPTER THREE

The start of the school year was slow. The teachers wearily made their way to class while the hall was over whelmed with adolescent noise. The overpowering smell of sweaty young boys filled the school. Boys looked like they were all arms and all legs. Girls had matured into their new bodies like a cocoon metamorphosing into a butterfly. Bells rang and life resumed itself in the newly painting walls of the old middle school.

Jenny helped Mary Beth off the bus and into the wheel chair. There had been some discussion about whether her condition merited a handicap privilege but the school principal erred on the side of caution. In other words, he would had rather let the perfectly healthy Mary Beth to use a wheel chair than risk a lawsuit. Jenny helped her to class each morning. She was glad to accompany her little sister. Jenny dared anyone to make fun of her or push her chair in any manner with a stern look that meant business.

Third period was Social Studies and the class had been let loose in the school library with their first project of the year. The students scattered, making noise with their little bit of freedom like marbles from a broken jar. Mr. Bragg liked for his students to learn on their own. He felt the teacher's role was to help kids find the information on their own, not stand in front of the class and talk. He had told them to write a report on a personal hero, someone in history, a musical artist or even a current celebrity. They could form a group of three, work in pairs of two or research the topic on their own.

Jenny preferred to work by herself. In the library, she went to the computer to search for articles. She put in the search words: DOG and RESCUE. After looking over the articles, she just shook her head. She put in another search: ANIMALS, HISTORY, RESCUE and found an article on Henry Bergh, the founder of the A.S.P.C.A: American Society of the Prevention of Cruelty to Animals. She printed out three long articles and paid the librarian two dollars. Jenny passed Katrina, the most talkative girl in her class.

The African American girl was tall for her age and was talking, full of energy. She always wore shorts and the most beautiful shirts and athletic shoes. Jenny liked her but found herself in trouble when she gathered in the crowd that followed Katrina. Katrina was searching for a female role model in contemporary music. She not only knew who her subject would be, but so did the whole class and the Algebra class across the hall. She yelled "Lil Kim!" Lil Kim is a current rapper.

"Shhhhhh." hissed the librarian.

Katrina flipped around and mocked the woman for a second and then began to lower herself into a chair.

Hiding in-between the shelves, Jenny sat down and began to read. She habit of dreaming about new books and new information. Jenny fought to keep her eyes open but it was useless. Nodding off, her head went to the side and the book fell to the side.

Jenny found herself walking in New York City during April of 1866. Buildings were close together and tall but there were no skyscrapers. Men and women gathered in the streets all making their way to their destination in haste. Some couples grappled on to each other, laughing and talking. There were buggies and horses everywhere. Women were dressed in dark, long skirts that flared out at the waist. Their waists were tiny. What lacked in the middle of their bodies was made up for on their heads. Huge, ornate bonnets were the style. They waltzed in and out of the crowd as if they were dancing. Mozart's symphonic music was to be heard in the background. (Jenny was one of the few students to actually listen to the odd tunes in Music Class.) Men wore dark suits with waist coats and pocket watches. They donned long handle bar mustaches and top hats. Among the men, was one man looking over the horses that were stopped, waiting for another fair. Jenny went up to the man who introduced himself as Henry Bergh.

"What are you doing?" asked Jenny. She walked beside him as he stroked the horses. "Checking the horses for ingrown harnesses. It's against the law, you know. What are you wearing?

Jenny looked down and saw she was dressed as a clown with bright red pants and oversized shoes. "What is an Ingrown Harness?" she asked as she looked at her hands which were covered with white gloves.

"The owners put the harnesses on when they are young and the horse grows. The harness becomes attached to the skin and is extremely painful."

They walked along the streets until they came upon an awful sight. A man was whipping his horse to death, literally. The poor beast leaned to the right and was foaming at the mouth. It's owner whipped it and cussed it. Women were crossing the street to avoid seeing the cruel actions of the dingy little man. They held their gloved hands to their eyes.

"Sir, sir. You are breaking the law and you must stop." said Henry Bergh to the man whipping the horse. The man ignored him.

"Sir, you probably do not realize it but the law of 1860 prevents any one from hurting an animal in such a way that it offends or *hurts the feelings* of the public. Look at the women hiding their eyes!" (The new law said that if someone hurts an animal and it offends another person, the animal owner can be fined.)

"Go to Hell!" yelled the horse owner. With an unexpected boldness, Bergh took the whip and called for police officers to come.

"What do you think you are doing, man." Bergh threw the whip behind him.

The carriage driver began sputtering.

"Just because you wear a expensive suit and hat, you think you can tell me my business. Give me back me whip now."

A man with a camera stood nearby and a low pop and smoke bellowed from the picture making devise. Bergh directed his attention to police officers which were coming in their direction. Traffic stalled on the New York street and the hustle of carriages and wagons came to a halt.

"What is going on?" said one horse taxi to another.

His answer was one name but that one name said volumes.

"Bergh."

Children gathered as the horse owner was taken away. Henry Bergh looked over the horse with a pitiful stare. An attractive woman came through the crowd and joined the onlookers and then went right up to Henry herself. It was Catherine, his wife. They looked over the beaten horse. There was no one around to help the animal. It went quietly out of the world, no thanks for all the work it had done.

"What are you going to do?" asked Jenny to Henry Bergh.

"Little girl, I think I will take my inherited millions and establish the first horse hospital in the city." said Bergh.

"If it is up to me, this will be the last horse to die in this horrid manner."

"Yes, that is most appropriate, dear." said Catherine, a tear rolling down her eye. Catherine turned to Jenny.

"You see, my husband, Henry has spent his whole life searching for a good cause to spend his money. He wanted to be a diplomat and ambassador to other countries from the United States but it did not work out."

"So, is he the founder of the American Society for the Prevention of Cruelty to Animals (A.S.P.C.A.)? asked Jenny.

"Yes, but his first and foremost concern are for the horses that are misused in the city. Dogs and cats come much later, many years into the future. Without the horse, Henry feels that this great country of ours would not be as far along as it is. He wants to give something back to the animals that fought in war and help build the Union Pacific Railroad. In Henry's mind, we owed a debt to the horse."

"Oh." said Jenny. She saw a young boy with newspapers in his hand. He wore a cap and had on short pants. He made his way through the crowd, passing out papers and collecting change. Henry, Catherine and the horse were gone. The boy yelled, "Read all about The Great Meddler. Read it here first, Henry Bergh and his personal mission with his fellow society dilettantes to save all horse and the cows from cruelty. Read all about it."

Daniel looked over the library shelf at Jenny asleep on the floor. He threw a wad of paper at her face.

"Hey!" yelled Jenny. She woke up, startled.

"We have to go back to class. Mr. Bragg is looking all over the place for you. He just called role." Jenny jumped to her feet. They both ran back towards the doors.

Born in 1813, Henry Bergh founded the ASPCA (American Society of the Prevention of Cruelty to Animals), over the misuse of horses. He felt we owed the horse a debt. In April of 1866, the first animal cruelty laws were passed due to Bergh.

Jenny worked on her report with all her free time and was ready to give it the following Monday.

With a flow chart behind her, Jenny's voice became shaky when reading her conclusion. Jenny had pictures of animals blown up on a copier and displayed them as she talked. A few kids began to squirm in their seats. Daniel stared at her intently, hanging on to every word. Jenny told the class about Henry Bergh and the poor horse he could not save and began talking about prevention.

"A lot of people say we put dogs "to sleep". That phrase is an euphemism. An euphemism is a nice word for the unpleasant, truthful word. To euthanize an animal means to kill it. Another euphemism for killing an animal is putting it down. I will use that term. In Henry Bergh's time, dog catchers were paid five cent a dog and would drown them in the river."

There was a collective "Ewww."

The word 'pound' in 'dog pound' came from colonial times. Stray farm animals, pigs or cows, were property, like cars. They would wonder off and were 'impounded'. Now, they are mostly for dogs and cats and pounds are now shelters. There are about five thousand in the United States. At one time, they used to use toxic gas to kill the unwanted animals. The public receives no information about it.

Jenny had drawn a map of North Carolina on poster board with blue and red counties. Red counties had large numbers of animals in shelters that did not find homes.

Jenny suddenly had to cough. She tried to hold it back but she could not go on talking.

"May I get some water?"

Zeb Lee, who sat in the back, yelled out, "She has had too much time. She's boring."

Daniel turned and gave him a dirty look. Zeb opened his arms and popped his eyes and said, "WHAT, are you going to start 'sumtum'?

Jenny cleared her throat and continued without noticing the conflict.

Zeb prepared spit balls and formed a weapon from his pen.

"If some people knew the truth, perhaps they would make more of an effort to spay or neuter their pets. Another problem is people adopt animals and do not how to train them when they grow up, so they toss them.

The shelter has remained unchanged for years. They need more room. Perhaps a pet tax would help. Not for non-animal owners, most pet people would not mind if it saved lives. People who fix their pets should pay the least, people who allow their dogs to have puppies should pay more, breeders should pay even more and pet farms or puppy mills should pay the most.

We need new ideas, like kill free shelters. In Wilmington, Friends of Felines, catch cats, spay and neuter the cats, tag them, and put them right back where they found them. We should appreciate the animals, from every guard dog to every lap kitty. My mother always said that the Bible said that God gave us dominion over the animals. We should all follow the example of Henry Bergh and take care of our ....OWW...animals." The first spit ball was a bull's eye.

Her report was almost over. With a hand shaking, Jenny rotated post cards. She felt the sting of a spit ball on her forehead. Zeb started a disruption. It would become the incident of the year.

Zeb jumped up on the back of his chair, his long legs pushing on the empty seat in front of him. No one wanted to sit by Zeb.

"Katrina's uncle gasses them cats! Yeah, he gasses them all day long. I hear he drinks and cries when he kills cats. I hate cats. Don't you Mr. Bragg?"

Zeb laughed, his eyes glared at the back of Katrina's head. Everyone stared at Zeb, then Katrina turned. The boy beside Katrina began closing his notebooks. He grabbed his coat and slid his desk as far away from Zeb and Katrina as he could.

Katrina's right fist balled up. Jenny turned to look at the teacher. Katrina, with the furious resolve of an lioness on a zebra hunt turned, pushed off her desk with her two back feet, slid her belly on Zeb's desk, her face in his. Wrapping her arms around his neck, as if seducing him, she moved closer to his face.

"I don't think my uncle cries when he kills cats...oh, he makes a sound, maybe like this!"

Katrina pulled his hair with all her might, pulled back her arm, her body lifting and moving as she aimed for Zeb's face and hit him, closed fist, square in the nose. He grabbed her neck and Katrina lowered her arm, grabbing him underneath the desk.

Zeb screamed and began to cry. Katrina let go and straightened up. She sat up proudly on Zeb's desk, wiping her hands as if as if to say, 'I'm done.' She smiled as she stared at him. No one talked about Katrina's family.

"Katrina, you may go to the chill out room. Zeb, if you are able you may report to the nurse." Mr. Bragg rose slowly to assert his authority.

"Katrina did the right thing, Mr. Bragg." said Daniel.

"You may join Katrina in the chill out room." Daniel slammed his book shut and got out of his seat. Jenny defended Daniel.

Mr. Bragg secretly agreed with both of them. He thought to himself. "If he was three I'd give him a smack on the rear but here he is nearly fifteen. What can be done now." Mr Bragg rose from his seat to maintain control in the classroom. Zeb could not take over. All the kids were watching the teacher.

"You may join them as well." Jenny's mouth fell open with shock. She was not used to being called down.

"Daniel is just voicing his opinion. If the teachers in the younger grades would have done something besides fill Zeb with candy and put him in the special class..." Jenny rose up and closed her books, packing away her presentation. Mr. Bragg leaned in, "Don't say special class, Miss Brown. The report is a sure 'A' Now, go quietly."

Zeb could be heard wailing down the hall.

"Who's crying now?" yelled Katrina.

Mr. Bragg used his "walky-talky". With Zeb in the halls, he did not want to risk sending Jenny, Daniel and Katrina out unescorted. The physical education teacher showed up. She was tall, heavy set and definitely not one to be questioned when she spoke. She escorted the three of them to chill out.

The chill out room was at the far end of the school. It was a plain room, no posters or decor. There were nine desks in the room. Some kids and teachers alike called it the Purgatory Palace. Purgatory is a euphemism for Hell.

Mrs. Eye, queen of the palace, sat on her throne at the front of the room and mostly read romance novels. She had bus duty and would often leave the children unattended at the end of the day. She was five months pregnant and thought the kids were old enough to dismiss their selves. Time was not wasted in chill out. Another student from the class brought their work and disciplinary papers. There had been students to sit in there for three months or more, refusing to work and their parents refused to come get them out. Jenny, Daniel and Katrina did not know how long they would be in chill out.

Jenny sat down and began doing her homework. Daniel slammed open his notebook and scribbled. Katrina laughed and talked to the teacher.

"When you going to have that baby?" asked Katrina to Mrs. Eye.

"I think we have a Christmas baby, just in time for Santa Claus." responded the teacher as she cradled her round stomach. She smiled and laughed with Katrina.

Jenny looked at Katrina and smiled.

"I am just curious, does your uncle really have to work at the animal shelter?"

Daniel gave Jenny a stare and his mouth fell wide open. He looked as if he did not believe his ears. Katrina could be made mad at the drop of a hat or rather a slam dunk by James Hudson, their seven foot basketball player.

Katrina, the mischief maker, walked by Daniel and yelled in his face, "BOO!". He acted like a frightened hermit crab, crab crawling in his desk back to the back of the room.

"Yes, since he was nineteen or so. He takes a lot of pride in his work." Katrina made sure that Mrs. Eye was not listening. "He is a very spiritual man. He cares for their sad little bodies, he prepares the souls. It is a gift. I do not think he is crazy but my daddy does."

"How?" asked Jenny.

In a whisper, Katrina continued.

"He buries the dogs and cats like humans, but they just supposed to be dumped. The cats have their own special place. There are more cats so two might share a grave. He owns about fifty acres back there."

"Fifty acres? Does your family live there too?" asked Jenny.

"No, this is not family land. Uncle Cletis inherited it from Marcus Rolland. He was the previous keeper of the animals, or their 'souls' as my uncle would say. Uncle Cletis took this position when Rolland died. I am not sure if Rolland gave him the gift or if my uncle was born with it and found Rolland." Katrina began to write down her assignments.

"What do you mean...gift? He is just burying cats and dogs, right?" asked Daniel.

Katrina laughed.

"You come with me and ask him. I have never seen it but he says he communes with their ghosts, their spirits once or twice a year. Some of these animals have come back to life a hundred times. They reincarnate, until they find someone to love them, then they follow that person into the afterlife."

Jenny and Daniel sat quiet and looked at each other. Katrina opened a book and began to write as if she had passed on ordinary school gossip. Mrs. Eye gathered her purse and struggled with her pregnancy to get out of the seat.

"Bus duty. You kids go on the third bell."

Katrina turned to Jenny and Daniel.

"You want to ask him for yourself, don't you? I been to chill out a lot, Mrs. Eye does not come back."

Katrina looked down the hall and headed out the glass doors to the field. Daniel lost his fear at the thought of an adventure and jumped from his seat and followed her.

"What if he is crazy?" asked Jenny asked Daniel with a hissing whisper.

"I don't know but I am going to get in major trouble any ways, might as well have fun." said Daniel with resignation. He shrugged and went to the glass doors chasing Katrina. Jenny shook her head and looked into her book. Then, she looked at the clock. She slammed the book shut and yelled

"Wait for me!" as she hit the glass door and burst out unto the back field behind the school, it would be the most important decision of her life.

CHAPTER FOUR

There was a dirt road that went past the school and Katrina seemed to know where she was going.

"My uncle will give me a ride home." said Katrina. "He works in his boneyard up on the hill. That is the area past the landfill."

"Will he take us home?" asked Jenny.

"Sure." Katrina laughed. She continued up the road. The three of them skipped and laughed and enjoyed the chilly, fall afternoon.

"My uncle is a little crazy. My mama said it was because he loves animals and he hates the way people treat them. He works in the animal boneyard."

"What is a boneyard?" asked Jenny. Jenny and Daniel glanced at each other and grimaced.

"It is what my Grandma calls a cemetery. Aunt Tee calls it a Bone Orchard, it is another word for cemetery. Burial grounds."

Daniel said, "That is awful."

"You don't think all the kitties and puppies get homes, do you?" asked Katrina, rolling her eyes at Daniel.

"Never thought about it until Jenny's report." said Daniel.

"Most people don't." said Katrina.

"Surely, some of dogs and cats get adopted?" asked Daniel.

"Yep, spring is best, puppies are in season. But some do like the holidays, that is when the breeders really make the cash. But in June, here come the big doggies, the Christmas present that grows."

They could see the landfill ahead but their sense of smell was their first clue that they were getting near. Katrina put a bandana around her face like a robber in the old west.

"What is that odor?" said Jenny. She wrinkled her nose.

"We must be getting near the landfill." said Daniel.

"I thought the animals were cremated." said Jenny.

Katrina slowed down a bit.

"He is not the only one that works there, but he is the boss. My daddy says that he is crazy! It was last Thanksgiving. We were all sitting around the table when my uncle says the animals come back to life when he is on the hill and it is a full moon."

"Is he dangerous crazy?" asked Jenny. She was ready to turn back.

"No. He's fine. I will get him to tell you." Katrina laughed. There seemed to be acres of trash. Jenny regretted following Daniel and Katrina. She just wanted to get home. Finally, the landfill ended and they were still on the dirt road surrounded by oaks and pines.

"See, there he is on that bulldozer." pointed Katrina. They ran all the way towards the figure who was getting off the bulldozer and wiping his forehead with his arm.

"Hello Lucy. How is my favorite niece?" asked the old man.

"It's Katrina! Dee Dee's girl. I thought I was your favorite, Uncle Celtis!"

"Who you got with you there, Bonnie and Clyde?"

Jenny decided he looked harmless. He was an older man with some gray hair on his head and in his beard. He wore overalls and white t-shirt underneath, although her father had warned her not to trust any stranger, but with two other children there, she felt safe.

"Uncle Cletis can you take me to the store on the way home. I am hungry." asked Katrina. Never having any children, Uncle Cletis was an easy touch for candy and soft drinks.

"Sure, your friends coming along too?" said the old man.

"Uncle Celtis, tell my friends about the dogs and cats."

"They don't want to hear about that." said her uncle.

"Yes, we do." said Daniel and Jenny in unison.

"Well, I am what is called a guardian. A guardian is someone who can hold the door open between the world we know and the world to come. I mean the afterlife." He paused and he saw Daniel and Jenny were hanging on every word.

"All dogs and all cats are reborn until they can serve a master who loves them. Their spirits clamor together and they wait to be reborn. If they are loved they can wait for their masters and not have to come back no more."

"Can you see a certain dog or cat that has passed away?" asked Jenny.

"Yes, my first dog, Bell, comes to visit me all the time. She is waiting for me. Ever see how a puppy wags his tail and begs to be loved?" asked Uncle Cletis.

"Yes." said Daniel.

"That is why. He or she knows she has to please and serve a master in order to be loved. It is the only way they can finally rest in the after-life. I feed them love through praying and chanting. Our family is from New Orleans and we have the gift to commune with the dead. I reassure them before they are reborn."

Jennifer walked around the place looking. It was beautiful. Stone slabs among boxwoods and other hedges that were meticulously cared for and hedged were squared off like a small town. Wind blew softly through wind chines. Jenny walked a little ways. It was quite peaceful. The carefully manicured trail led from one garden to the other. There were benches made of wood from orange crates. Large statues of dogs and cats, as well as tiny glass figurines, plants of all types, rocks and other decorative items were places in each twelve foot by twelve foot square in a most pleasing way.

"Can we go now?" asked Katrina.

"Yeah, come on. Get in the car." said Uncle Cletis.

All three kids ran toward his old car.

Katrina yelled, "Dibs, I got the front seat!"

They ran over to his car, a 1989 Pontiac Grand Am. Daniel fell into the backseat and said, "Dude, the eighties called and wants their car back." The hood was solid blue and it was as large as a queen size bed. Four large people could sit on it.

"It gets me to work and back and that's all I need. Katrina, you pick one of your guest to sit up front. You know my sister, your mama, gave you better manners."

Uncle Celts opened the door and slid behind the steering wheel.

"Got to give it some gas." He tried to crank his old car but it would not turn over.

"Speaking of gas, is that how the pound kills the unadoptable dogs and cats?" asked Daniel.

Celtis stopped short and turned to look at Daniel.

"Yes, but things are getting better. We use shots now. The other man does it so he leaves this job to me. I have the harder job but I have to bury them proper or they may get lost in the after-life. No one knows why I want this job. It is a secret. If you don't mind, keep this to yourself. The kids would just tease Katrina and her mother would be on my door step."

Katrina had her hands behind her, whistled and looked at the sky. She seemed a little embarrassed.

Jenny walked away while Cletis tried to get the car started. She looked around and there were carefully cultivated gardens everywhere. A white cat rubbed itself against a decorative stone not far from Jenny.

"Here Kitty, Kitty." As she walked toward the cat, it kept away from her. It vanished behind a stone.

Cletis sighed when the car finally started and he waved for Jenny to come get in the car. She ran and hopped in the back seat.

"These woods go on for miles. Every seven years, I start over up here but there are graves almost all the way to Pitt county." said Uncle Cletis. "But I wish more people would pay for their dogs and cats to be fixed. There is no need for this place."

"I think it is wonderful... the way it is like a human cemetery." said Jenny, "And that you care for them. How did you come to know Marcus Rolland?"

Uncle Celtis looked at her, surprised.

"I don't rightly know. I was drawn here. He asked me to come up at midnight on a full moon. I was about sixteen. I was tired of school. I felt like I had nothing to lose. Mr. Rolland's was well known. Everyone spoke well of him. It was almost one o'clock in the morning by the time I made it up here. Mr. Rolland's looked at his watch and said we were too late. Just as we started to leave, a small white cat came up to my feet. It stroked my legs, you know, the way cats do to mark their territory. Then, I saw them coming from a light in the woods. Hundreds of them. Some seemed to run slow, some fast. They were strangely quiet. They faded in and out. Mr. Rolland looked at me and asked, 'Do you see a cat?' I barely croaked out a 'yes'. He said 'I see you already see all of them. I am most certain you have the gift and this is your destiny.'"

Jenny started to tell about the cat but feared ridicule from Katrina and Daniel so she thought about Tater and wondered if the dog was loved enough to wait for her.

"Could we stop by the store on the way home and get some drinks at the store?" asked Katrina. Daniel smiled and piled in the back seat beside Katrina.

The car whined and finally, with a roar, the engine turned over. It was loud. Jenny found the old fashioned seat belt and fastened it with a click.

"Did you have any more pets, Mr. Cletis?" asked Daniel.

"Sure, I had a lab named Pal She was a chocolate lab and live nearly fifteen years. I see her from time to time. She is waiting for me on the other side." said Cletis with a smile.

Daniel and Katrina just looked at each other and shrugged.

"I wish they all found homes." Jenny said.

Celtis turned. "We do too, young lady. Sometime we adopt them all out. But then, there are some weeks no one comes in. There are a lot of people out there trying to help. The prison up in Jackson takes eight dogs every three months. They train them and they get adopted miles away, some all the way to New York."

"I wish there was something we all could do." said Jenny.

"Tell your friends to have their dogs fixed. Cats too. If there are no puppies, then there will be no unwanted dogs." said Uncle Cletis.

"But people do want them. Right?"

"Some think they want a puppy, then it grows into a big dog. These dogs can live up to ten or fifteen years. Little dogs live longer."

Katrina butted in. "Aunt Matilda has this little Maltese dog that is twenty one. Nothing but hair and teeth." Daniel and Jenny laughed. They both wanted Katrina as a friend.

Uncle Cletis laughed. "That little dog will bite the head off a Pitt Bull!"

Jenny was still concerned about the animals in the shelter.

"The second biggest reason dogs come in is there not "socialized" properly. People will get a dog, keep it on a chain, a kid runs up and pulls it's tale. Chomp! Kid screams. Puppies and dogs need to trust their owner and be around children with adults telling them not to tease the dog. They need to meet other dogs and people, especially when they are young."

The car pulled into the Mini-mart. Katrina opened the car door before Cletis was able to stop.

"Katrina, you settle down and act like you got some sense. Sit in that seat until we stop."

Katrina closed the door and looked down at her hands. In her excitement, she forgot that Uncle Celtis could really embarrass her in from of her class mates.

Jenny got out. She walked in the store and picked out a soda for her sister. Daniel got a candy bar and Katrina picked out an ice cream. She stopped and went back and got one for herself. Uncle Celtis drove Daniel home first and then went by Jenny's house.

"I am really interested in dogs. Can I talk to you again?" asked Jenny.

"Surely, you may." said Uncle Celtis.

"Oh, and I like your white cat. She is pretty." said Jenny.

"You saw a white cat! said Uncle Cletis with a surprised tone.

"Thank you for the ..." Jenny's voice trailed as they pulled up to her house. It was obvious that her world was about to be turned upside down.

CHAPTER FIVE

Jenny gathered her book bag and felt her heart pound as she saw an unfamiliar car and a moving van in her driveway. Mary Beth was in her wheelchair in the front yard, crying.

"Jenny! We have to share a room now, Linda Kaye is moving all your stuff in my room! And they opened Mom's room!"

"What?!" yelled Jenny. The thought of her private things being handled by Linda Kaye made her see red.

Jenny walked into her home feeling as if she could slap someone. Jenny was not one to back down from a fight.

Ms. Vivian was putting her things on the couch. Linda Kaye popped a bubble as she dumped Jenny's books unto the floor by the couch.

"Where's my Dad?" asked Jenny.

Ms. Vivian stopped. To Jenny, she seemed larger than she remembered. Ms. Vivian had three layers of eye make-up. Her nails were long, fake and fancy. She looked at Jenny as if sizing her up for a snack.

"Hello, Jennifer. Linda Kaye has told me all about you. Your dad says you are a smart girl. Be smart."

Ms. Vivian's icy stare gave Jenny the willies. "Help us out and this could go down a lot easier, especially for your sister."

"Why is my sister crying in the front yard?" asked Jenny with a firm, defiant voice.

"Your sister is overly sensitive. Ignore her. She is just crying for attention." answered Ms. Vivian.

"I'm not touching anything until I talk to my father. I will be in the front yard with my sister."

Jenny turned on her heal and slammed the front door. She went to her sister and brushed away the tears.

"It will be O.K. Let them do all the work. I want you to meet somebody." said Jenny.

"Who? I have met enough people today." said Mary Beth through her sniffles. Jenny pushed her wheel chair on the paved road and headed for Mr. Quinn's. She turned back and glared at Ms. Vivian who shook her head as she stared out the door. Jenny could hear Ms. Vivian and Linda Kaye argue.

"Linda Kaye, let's go ahead and fix the room, she's not going to help."

"That's not fair!" Linda Kaye shouted.

"Who said any of this was fair." She gave her daughter the same frozen look which prompted Linda to careful pick up the books she had just dumped and began to arrange them neatly.

Jenny pushed the chair unto the gravel. Mary Beth carefully got up and held on to Jenny. She preferred to hold on to the right side of a person to walk. She could walk fine along the side of the house, if they took it slow.

"You want to meet Tater?" said Jenny to her little sister, hoping it would stop the tears. They walked slowly down to Mr. Quinn's house.

"Wow, is that Tater? I have never seen a dog so big!"

Tater was dancing around and bounding on the leash. She barked really loud. The Great Dane was massive compared to most dogs.

"Yep. I have been working with her every day. You are going to walk her." said Jenny.

"Are you crazy, no!" said Mary Beth.

Jenny went and let loose Tater. She bounded for Mary Beth who defensively put her arms around her own face. Tater came to a halt in front of Mary Beth.

"Sit!" said Jenny. Tater sat. She looked back and forth between Jenny and Mary Beth. Jenny put a leash on Tater and pulled her beside Mary Beth. Tater's back was the perfect height for Mary Beth to lean on. Mary Beth caressed the dog in wonder and leaned her right arm over Tater's back. Some dogs have a sense when people are disabled. They make good therapy dogs. Mary Beth and Tater fit like a hand in a glove. It had been forever since Mary Beth had taken a walk outside.

Jenny was happier and hoped Mary Beth would remember the day as perfect outdoor walk in the cool, fall air, instead of the day Linda Kaye took over her world. Jenny and Mary Beth waited until the last bit of light set over the pine trees before they went back home.

Before going in, Jenny took a deep breath. She steeled herself for any blow that Ms. Vivian or her daughter could give out. To their pleasant surprise a pizza box was on the kitchen table. Mary Beth reached for a piece when Jenny gently pulled her hand away.

"Ms. Vivian...are you here?"

Ms. Vivian came out of the bathroom. She had on a pink, purple and red robe. Jenny whispered to Mary Beth, "the circus is in town."

"If you ever walk out on me again without telling me where you are going, giving me the most basic courtesies of saying 'goodbye', I will make it my mission to take away all the freedom you ever thought you had."

She turned and went into their father's bedroom.

"You may eat the left over pizza. There is salad in the refrigerator."

Jenny reached past the box. There was a note on the table.

"Dear Jenny and Mary Beth: I have gone on to work. This situation is temporary. Please do as Vivian ask you to do. In the long run, she is doing us a big favor. I will be home on Saturday. Be good. Love, Dad."

Jenny read the letter to her sister.

"If he loved us he would have told us when big old lard butt and her teenage mutant ninja hot pants would be moving into our home."

They laughed. Jenny and Mary Beth wolfed the rest of the pizza down and then made their way into their crowded bedroom. The little white poodle jumped on Jenny's bed.

"Hey, what is your name?" The small, white poodle rolled on her back and begged for attention. She petted the dog.

"Maratee!" The voice wavered from Jenny's old bedroom. Jenny could hear crying. She gathered her bathrobe and shuffled into her bedroom shoes. As the poodle went into the room, Jenny knocked and entered to see Linda Kaye crying on the side of her bed. Her hair was wet, one side dark and one side light. The purple hair tint was combed back.

"What's wrong?" asked Jenny.

Linda Kaye got up and closed the door motioning for Jenny to sit on the bed. In a hushed voice she opened up to Jenny.

"Sorry about getting your room." said Linda Kaye.

"That's okay. We have the largest room now, it was our father and mother's room. We feel closer to her that way." Jenny offered a smile. Linda Kaye nodded.

"My mom found out I went to see Nick yesterday. You know, Nick in Spanish? He sits toward the back. Anyways we are going out and Mom says I can't date until next year. I have to be in high school. We have been meeting at the Porter house."

A shocked look came over Jenny's face. Nick was older, sixteen and still in middle school because of being held back. He was one of those boys who were naturally good looking. His brown hair was thick in the front but he had it combed back. She met him on the school bus when he and his family had moved down from New York. He had rugged good looks and was known as a bad boy. He would stop at each seat and say "Move ober." Jenny let him share her seat.

"You go out with Nick?" asked Jenny. And before Linda could answer, "The Porter house! You have really been there?" asked Jenny.

"Oh, many times." remarked Linda Kaye with an air of accomplishment.

Maratee jumped up on the bed.

"She is a cute dog." commented Jenny.

"Her name is Maratee Rochelle Small. That is her full pedigree name. Look at her pictures." Linda looked under the bed and took out a scrapbook. In the scrapbook were pictures of herself, Maratee and ribbons. Mary Kaye had a show dog that was a winner. The ribbons were mostly red. Maratee had yet to win the elusive blue ribbon. First place.

"I take care of a Great Dane," said Jenny. She heard herself lie. "...for money." She did not know why she lied.

"Great. I can show you training techniques."

Jenny and Linda Kaye made friends that night but only at home, not at school. Linda Kaye's popularity ruled in the halls and she would only nod at Jenny. Jenny did not care. She had her hands full looking after Mary Beth and Tater.

Originally from Germany, there are three size of poodles, first of all the Standard poodle with was used for hunting water fowl, then later miniature and toy. Poodles do not shed which has made them popular, but need to be combed often as their fur matts. Coming in all colors, poodles are very smart and active, which mean they need a lot of attention.

CHAPTER SIX

Jenny stared at the large oyster, a grey, slimy blob, that her father waved in front of her face. She watched Ms. Vivian, now Mrs. Brown feed her father an oyster and he feed her one. Her whole body shuttered. She looked at Linda Kaye and Mary Beth. They ate their shrimp plates without noticing their parents. Jenny thought back to the beginning of the weekend. The plan for her father to marry Ms. Vivian became a sudden blur of shopping for ugly dresses and phone calls.

George came home on Friday night with a big bouquet of flowers.

"Let's tie the knot, honey. I called your boss and the preacher. Sunday is available!"

On Sunday, George and Ms. Vivian were married at the little Baptist church which was about a mile down the road. It was a cinder block building painted white. The doors were red. The family used to go there and the girls were both baptized in a portable baptism pool. The pastor had resided over Sandra's funeral.

"What a happy occasion." said the small pastor. He had on a black suit. The girls had three matching dresses that they would never wear again and held hand-picked flowers. Ms Vivian's boss had brought his camera and Ms. Vivian wanted pictures. It was a small wedding, mostly co-workers from George and Vivian's jobs were there. Aunt Mamie came but George had to pick her up and take her home.

After the service, the pastor invited the new family to church.

"I work most Sundays." said Ms. Vivian in a flat tone.

After the service, they all went out to eat seafood. There was a big red velvet cake made by a co-worker from the quarry. Mary Beth stuffed hush puppies in her pocket book for Tater and Maratee.

On Monday, George returned to work and the girls fell back into a routine. Jenny found she had more free time as the chores were divided three ways. She no longer had to cook. Ms. Vivian worked two shifts but was home to make the evening meal. They ate together as a family.

One afternoon, Jenny called Daniel on her cell phone. She sat on the back porch steps crouched as if it provided more privacy. Linda Kay seemed to know everything and this she wanted to keep secret.

"I have seen Linda Kay training Maratee for the dog show. Will you help me train Tater? Meet me at Tater's house in fifteen minutes. Bring that fishing pole of yours." said Jenny.

"Fishing pole? We going to the river?"

"No. Cut off the hooks but have a long line. I'll show you." Jenny hung up. She quickly went into the kitchen slamming the door. She approached the refrigerator and looked to the left and to the right. She took out a pack of hot dogs and closed the door. Linda Kay was standing there, hold her cell phone in one hand texting. She looked at Jenny.

"What are you doing with those?"

"Nothing." said Jenny, she was startled.

"I am going to tell Mom." Linda Kaye retorted.

"Do, and I will tell her what you and your boyfriend do at the Porter house?"

"She will not believe you." Linda Kaye flipped back her hair and crossed her arms in defiance. They had been skipping class and making their way up the hill.

Jenny pressed on. "She may not believe me, true, but your after school extra-curricular activities might be worth a second look."

Linda Kaye did not want to mess up her fun and free afternoons with Nick. She had told her mother that she was in the Spanish Club but actually was meeting her boyfriend. Linda did not know if Jenny was bluffing but she did not want to push her luck.

"Mom trusts me. Keep the hot dogs, I hate them anyways."

"Well, that's between you and the 'mother of the year'." said Jenny as she slammed the back door.

Linda Kaye's face turned red. "I'm telling!" she squealed.

Mary Beth wheeled up beside Jenny. She has heard the argument over her Saturday morning cartoons.

"What are you doing?" she asked.

"Daniel and I are going to train Tater to be in the dog show? Don't tell Ms. Vivian."

"Can Tater come here to live? I like Tater." pleaded Mary Beth.

"If we get her trained, maybe Ms. Vivian will like her more." answered Jenny.

"Unless you take me this attempt of yours is going to be a disaster." commented Linda Kaye.

"Why?" asked Jenny.

"Watch me prepare to walk Maratee." said Linda Kaye.

"Maratee!!" called Linda Kaye.

The poodle came scrambling. It's nails clicked on the hardwood floors.

"ACCT!! CALMIT (calm it)" said Linda Kaye firmly.

Immediately, the poodle screeched to a stop and sat, panting. Her eyes were on Linda Kaye.

"When Mom let me have a puppy, the man who raised poodle pups told me to pick one that was not as playful as the others. I could not figure out why. The playful ones were so cute. He said, 'them pups are going to be harder to train, look at white one curled up in a ball sleeping. If I wanted a dog for a show, I'd pick her.' So I did."

"Before a walk, she has to be calm. This is just a little poodle. What are you going to do if you can't handle a Great Dane?"

"We will figure it out." said Jenny. "Know-it-all" said Jenny, under her breath. With that she took the package of hot dogs and ran out the door.

Both Daniel and Jenny met at the same time in front of old man Quinn's house. They laid their bikes down in front and went to the back. Tater began jumping and barking. She wagged her stump of a tail in anticipation of the morning treat.

"Tater needs to prance beside me and hold her head up. Then she has to stand and perfectly still with her head up. I have to jog her in a big circle."

"I still don't get this fishing pole." said Daniel.

"Her head needs to be held high. Tie a piece of a hot dog bit at the end of the pole and hold it right above her head as we walk. Make sure there are no hooks on that pole."

"I cut them off." said Daniel. After stringing the hot dog chunks at the tend of the line Daniel and Jenny went back to greet the excited dog.

"See girl." Jenny fed Tater one and put one on the end of the pole. Daniel held the pole too low and Tater gobbled the hot dog off.

"How I am supposed to hold the pole?" said Daniel perplexed.

"Boys, honestly if you had brains, you'd be dangerous." said Jenny. "I will hold the line and you walk Tater. She will learn to walk with her head high. Say 'heal' and keep her close to your side."

Jenny turned toward Tater who was wagging her tail and strained at the chain. Jenny was nervous inside but mimicked Linda Kaye. She held out her hand and said "Calm down.". With that, Daniel nodded and unlatched the chain from Tater's collar. The dog bolted forward and knocked Jenny down. Tater ate all the hot dog pieces at once.

"Hold her!" yelled Jenny.

"She is too strong." said Daniel. "I am going to put this leash latch around my waist. I'll show you who doesn't have brains." Tater looked back and saw Daniel. He tugged and Tater took off like a shot in the dark.

"OH, NO!" yelled Daniel. "GET THIS LEASH OFF…"

He could not say much before he hit the ground. Tater had realized she could pull and ran full force across the field. Jenny ran after them.

"Tell her to be 'CALM' !" yelled Jenny, running with all her might to catch up.

Daniel ate up a tall weeds and grass before Tater bolted into the wooded area. He plowed the field like a runaway tractor.

"TATER!" yelled Jenny.

The old man had opened the back door to see what the screaming was all about and broke into gut busting laughter. He held his side, smiling and chuckling.

After mowing down a bush, all hopes of dignity were lost for Daniel. His pants were around his knees. The limbs of the sharp edged limb had ripped his underwear in a horrifying manor. It did not free Daniel but his butt was exposed. The bruised and bashed boy tried to maneuver his feet so he would provide friction to gain control. He looked up and his eyes grew wide.

'NOT THE SWAMP!" These were his last words before he swallowed what tasted really bad. It was boggy, swamp water. Tater splashed through it in bounds.

Jenny finally caught up with the dog and grabbed hold of the leash and pulled. Tater stopped and went over to Daniel who was spitting and wiping his face. Tater began licking his face all over and Jenny laughed.

"It ain't funny." Daniel yelled. Covered with swamp water and mud, he turned quickly so Jenny could not see his buttocks. He pulled out his shirt which covered his torn jeans.

"It is not funny. 'Ain't' is not a word. It was beyond funny. It was hilarious." Jenny had to bite her lip before she wounded any more male pride.

Linda Kaye had jumped the ditch and was walking toward them. She had a leash in her hand.

"Oh great." said Jenny. Daniel hurried to make sure his T-shirt was pulled over his torn pants and he made a useless attempt to clean his shirt with his hands.

"So this is Tater." The moment Linda Kaye, taller than Jenny or Daniel snapped the leash on the dog, she sat down. She held the collar up with a firm grasp.

With the collar and leash firmly in her hand, Linda Kaye said, "Walk."

Tater tried to pull her but Linda Kaye blocked her and made her sit again.

"CALMIT." said Linda Kaye, loud and firm.

When the dog relaxed her muscles and did not pull on the leash, Linda Kaye fed her a treat.

"Again, walk." This time Tater stayed by her side. The three of them walked back to the old man's house. They had to stop once, to calm Tater.

While Linda Kaye unwrapped the dog's chain and Daniel fetched some water in a bucket, Jenny approached the old man. He stood holding his dirty door with a window busted out and chipped paint open. Flies were sailing past his head.

"That was some show, boy." He laughed hard.

Daniel turned as red as the old broke down tractor in the weeds.

"I, I mean, we would like to train Tater to be in a dog show." said Jenny to the old man.

"If she wins first in place, you got to sell her and give me the money. Hold out for a good price. If she loses, you get to keep her." Old man Quinn loomed on the porch in the headquarters of his junk empire.

"What is a good price?" asked Daniel as Jenny looked over the papers.

"Start high, say four hundred. You can always go down but you can't go up if you start low." He scratched at his waist and shifted his hat. His paternal instincts took over.

"That is the most important rule in life kids, remember me telling you. You can always go down in price but never go up. You'll need that info when you start selling stuff." He smiled. He handed Jenny Tater's pedigree papers.

"Octave Juliet Barstow? What a name!" exclaimed Jenny.

"All them show dogs got funny names." sputtered the old man. He walked over and gave the dog an affectionate rub.

"I hope you get something, some kind of ribbon and junk like that." Quinn cleared his throat and closed the door.

"Now you have to take her home and get Ms. Vivian to let her stay." said Daniel.

"Can I keep her at your house?" asked Jenny.

"No way, my dad would make my butt into a hat." replied Daniel.

"Until I get our Mom's permission, can she stay here, Mr. Quinn?" asked Jenny.

"Sure but you feed and water her. The bag's on the porch."

Jenny had to face Ms. Vivian about Tater. She would need Linda Kaye on her side. It would be a miracle if her step-mom would allow Tater to stay.

CHAPTER SEVEN

The next morning, Ms. Vivian had cooked a full breakfast with pancakes. She left around noon. It was a Saturday.

"Linda. Let me do your turn to do the dishes." said Jennifer after supper. Ms. Vivian was a great cook but left a lot of dishes.

"Nope. You are on your own with Tater."

Jenny began organizing the plates.

"If I did some of your homework, you could spend a little more time with Nick". Jenny said.

"Are you out of your mind?" said Linda, who moved over and resumed doing dishes.

"There has to be a way! Mary Beth gets out of her chair and walks when she is around Tater. The dog has been chained out her whole life. Tater can help Mary Beth and we can help her." said Jennifer.

The two girls headed out after the dishes. As they approached the Quinn property, Jenny handed Linda the leash. Both girls sat on the back porch thinking about the situation. Finally, Linda sighed and said, "If you get Mary Beth up and walking with the dog, let me handle Mom."

Jenny hugged her and ran to get Tater. The dog bounded up and down with excitement. Tater wagged her tail as the girls put a leash on her and headed for the house.

"Calm it." said Linda Kaye. Tater responded well to Linda's commands and there was very little pulling headed toward home.

Entering the house, Jenny called out, "Mary Beth! MARY BETH! Come look here, we have a surprise!"

Tater looked to the right and left and perked up her ears as Mary Beth came rolling up in her wheel chair.

Jenny let the dog go to her sister.

"Tater! Can we keep her?" asked Mary Beth. The dog licked her face and stood as if to give Mary Beth support. Linda picked up the yapping Maratee, quickly. "It is best to introduce the dogs in the back yard." she said.

Outside, Maratee charged and Tater growling. Linda Kaye dropped to her knees.

"ACCT!" She put her hand in front of Maratee. She made sure her dog was calm and Tater smelled the poodle. Maratee began to run in large circles around Tater. Tater barked and put her front paws down and her butt in the air, wagging. Maratee jumped and bounced off the side of Tater. Mary Beth clapped. The sight of a small white poodle bouncing off Tater's side made the girls laugh. The dogs were barking up a storm and seemed to get along fine, Beth took the leash and, while leaning on Tater, walked in a circle following Linda who had leashed Maratee. She began taking her through show paces. Jennifer, playing guard duty watched for Ms. Vivian and soon saw the white Cadillac turn the corner.

"Linda! Your Mom is home!" yelled Jenny. As the girls, went to pick up the back yard, running in circles to hide the hundred and twelve pound Great Dane.

Ms. Vivian was getting out of the car and Jenny raced to catch her before she could see Tater. She stopped short as a man came from the yard next door. Jenny hid behind the bush and listened,

The man was their new neighbor, Mr. Alfred Snodgrass. The girls had been so busy they had not noticed the new neighbor moving in the finished house next door. He was a man with a head full of grayish black hair and a beard. He spoke with a slight accent that Jenny could not make outs.

"He is fat." said Mary Beth.

"Shhhh..." Jennifer answered.

All three girls listened from behind the side of the house.

"Are those your children with the dogs in the backyard?"

Ms. Vivian strolled around around the car, placed a hand on her hips, lowered her sunglasses. She sized up Alfred Snodgrass with a glare. She moved very close to Mr. Snodgrass, making him stumble slightly. The man cleared his throat and began again.

"Hello, I am your new neighbor, Alfred, Alfred Snodgrass. We at Forest Lawn Estates are forming a committee and one of the ordinances we wish to address is the barking of dogs. Also, the size of that dog." He paused to grimace and shake his head." Is it possible that you could have your pets hidden by a large white fence, not chain link like the one you have but perhaps a large white-picked fence. Please restrain your pets from making noise. That dog is so large." Snodgrass pointed a finger in Ms. Vivian's face.

The girls gasped all a once.

"I will call the police on those heathen girls of yours and their barking dogs..." Ms. Vivian grabbed his finger and pulled it backwards. Snodgrass screamed.

"Let go!"

"One. This is not Forest Lawn Estates. Two. you don't mess with my girls or," Ms. Vivian paused and glared at the fence behind their house...or their dogs. If we decide to have cats, birds or an elephant in the backyard, it is our business. Now go home or I'll break it clean off."

"Let go! I am calling the authorities!"

"Call Henry, call Jesse. The men you think going to have your back, I done been fixing coffee for them come twenty years."

"O.K. O.K. Let's start over."

"You get out my face and we will start over again when I want to start over again." She pushed him a side. "I need to talk to my family. Leave." she commanded

Snodgrass' voice became high pitched, his face, beet red.

"There were no dogs here when I bought the old house across the street. I can't have barking day and night. Those are the rules of Forest Lawn Estates!"

Ms. Vivian's attention had turned from Alfred Snodgrass to the activity in her back yard. She dismissed him with a wave of her hand. He may have been still talking when she walked to the side of the house.

She saw Mary Beth, up on her feet and moving fast by holding on to the Great Dane's back.

"Jennifer Antoinette Brown. NOW!" boomed Ms. Vivian.

Now in the world of kid-dom, how you were called, determined your current status with your parent and how much trouble you were in. If you were called by your nick-name, your parents were happy with you and most likely wanted you to perform some task. The mention of the first, second and last name indicated that you were in trouble, but the use of the word, "now", meant that you had violated a serious rule. In the south, the first and second named were often used in a casual, even affectionate manner.

Jennifer and Linda Kaye ran up to Ms. Vivian, blabbering.

Ms. Vivian did not hear a word. She was quite angry at first but she had calmed down when she observed Mary Beth walking, holding on to the Dane's back.

"I'll be," she said to herself, shaking her head, "all the therapists, all the doctors didn't do that child any good, but a dog has got her on her own two legs."

The sight of Mary Beth walking with the Great Dane was remarkable. Ms. Vivian thought of her husband and how wonderful it would be if George came home to a walking Mary Beth. Oh, yes, she would act offended at the dog's presence but give in after some rules were laid down, the mutt could stay.

The girls went in the house with the dogs through the back door. Ms. Vivian walked in and saw Tater. Their eyes momentarily locked and then Tater ran into the girls' room and tried to hide behind the bed. Her head was under the bed but the rest of her body stuck out, making them all giggle.

Jenny and Linda continued babbling about Tater and Ms. Vivian silenced them with a look. She walked in the house and saw Mary Beth, out of her chair, sitting beside the dog, petting him and laughing.

"You should have asked before bringing it up from the old man's house. But I guess it can stay. Must be fed and walked. It can sleep on the back porch. Dog prints on the floor will be cleaned right away. We are going to have to ask your father about getting shots from the vet. Dogs cost money. The dog food is coming out of your allowance."

The sight of Mary Beth laughing softened Ms. Vivian. She leaned against the door and smiled. The girls cheered and danced in a circle.

"It's got to be cleaned if it is going to come in this house." commanded Ms. Vivian. The girls made an afternoon of filling a play pool with bubble bath and cleaned both dogs, Great Dane and Poodle together. They laughed and yelled. Tater barked with a low pitch and Maratee with a high pitched yap.

Jenny ran outside. She saw the fat man and a short woman with frizzy hair. She turned and watched them from the porch.

"Dogs run away all the time." said the short woman to the fat man. They turned and walked away.

The wheelchair was not used for the rest of the evening. Mary Beth held on to walls and walked slowly but she walked on her own. Ms. Vivian went down to talk to Mr. Quinn. The girls got their supper ready and picked up the place. They were sitting at the table when Ms. Vivian returned.

"Mr. Quinn passed away." she said. "I spoke to the neighbor. Sometime during the day, the gas man found him clutching his chest.

Ms. Vivian turned in early and the girls let Tater off the porch, but her whines were keeping them up. Jenny and Mary Beth went to bed early too. Tater wedged himself down Mary Beth's leg on the bed, there was barely room for both of them, he licked her toes and she giggled herself to sleep.

Breakfast was a little chaotic. Ms. Vivian sat in the easy chair, delegating all the work to the three girls, while holding her coffee cup out when it needed to be filled. She giggled openly at the dogs begging for food and Mary Beth struggling with a thirty pound bag of dog food, her own child working the toaster and putting plates on the table. Jenny had learned to scramble eggs with her father. She was at the grill. There was a contented smile on Mary Beth's face. She walked without the wheel chair that day and the next day too.

Service dogs help disabled people live. Mary Beth was unable to walk after the accident, however, Tater gave her the confidence to try. Great Danes are the largest breed and are known as gentle giants. Bred to fight boars in the 1700s, the ears were clipped to keep from being torn. Great Dane's ears are naturally floppy.

CHAPTER EIGHT

Jenny, Daniel and Katrina made a habit of walking to Uncle Celtis' secret animal "boneyard" from school. They left school at three thirty and walked along the rural road for a mile. Today, it was a long walk but a pretty afternoon for the end of October. The smell of burning leaves filled the air and there was a thundercloud on the horizon. Daniel walked in the middle and listened to the girls, both taller than he and on each side. Sometimes, he would take a gander at the swampy ditches which were over grown with cat tails. He poked at frogs and turtles. Despite his pleas for attention, the girls would ignore him. Most days, Uncle Cletis was working but some days he would go home early and the kids would go there, as it was not that far.

They would arrive at Uncle Celtis' house around four. His neighborhood had stood for years and most of the people had great pride in their porches, lawns and mailboxes. Celtis, who was in his sixties, would greet them at the door. Katrina was interested in candy and other snacks, Daniel asked to watch the television and Jenny wanted to know about his pets, the mysterious animal spirits on his land in the woods beyond the county dump.

Uncle Celtis poured Jenny a soda and offered her some cookies.

"Do you see the spirits every day?" asked Jenny, munching on a ginger snap.

"No, not every day. Mostly near full moons."

"Do the dogs and cats fight?"

Uncle Cletis laughed.

"Sometimes there is a hiss or a brief chase, but they disappear into the spirit realm." Celtis thought for a minute. He scratched his gray hair and beard.

"They mostly need love. You see, if they have love in the waking life, they will be with the ones they loved throughout eternity, but if they are not loved, they return."

"How many times?" asked Jenny.

"As many times as it takes until they find the right master. A puppy or a kitten is at the mercy of chance and there are just too many to be loved like a family member. Some never know nothing but pain and hunger."

Jenny munched and drank her soda.

"What if they are loved only for a little while, not by the ones that own them but by a neighbor or a kid like me?"

"If they feel the bond, they will pass over and not have to return."

Each day, Jenny learned more and more about the afterlife and the life that awaited humans and creatures alike. She read books and watched any documentary about life after death. She gravitated toward Uncle Celtis and Daniel followed.

One day, Daniel asked Uncle Cletis, "Do you know of any human ghost?"

"The county has a few. But my gift is limited, I have only heard of ghost. And, of course, the little girl in white. I saw her three times.

"Where?" asked Katrina.

"Up in the woods, past the new Forest Lawn houses, is the old Porter house, as you know."

"I knew that place was haunted." exclaimed Daniel.

Jenny remained silent but her heart raced.

Uncle Cletis settled into the story and the kids just sit around him, listening.

"The Porters used to own all the land, all. They were an old family that farmed cotton. Most of the cotton you see within two miles of that place is owned and farmed by someone who moved to the central part of the state years and years ago. Rumor says it is Sam and Molly Porter's nephew. He was not there the night of the fire and the no one that knows what happened to Adlane, Molly's young niece.

It was Christmas when Adlane arrived. 1889. Molly's brother, Samuel had sent the young child to live with them and felt that the holidays would be more pleasant for her in her new home. Molly had really 'put on the dog'. Round here, that meant she went all out. The happy mother cooked a big turkey, a ham and had prepared pies and cakes for the arrival of Adlane. She had two boys but this was her chance to raise a girl. Sam had bought all the children clothes and toys but had a special doll for Adlane. It was a very happy time in that house."

No one knows how the fire started, the house was gutted in the back by the time the neighbors got the fire wagon up the road. Family died in their beds. Smoke inhalation. All the bodies were found except for Adlane's. Her body was never found. The oldest boy had no explanation and did not seem be concerned about Adlane's disappearance.

There was a huge search, in the woods, in the house but it has always been a mystery. Some say she went outside but why did she not come up when the crowds were putting out the fire? Some say they can see her in the woods around the house at night. It is as if she is still waiting for that Christmas morning. I have been up there a few times. I have seen her. She's waiting on her Christmas present to pass on. I have it. A doll, passed on to me by my family."

"Maybe, she is like the animals, needing love to move on." said Jenny.

"Yep, I think your right." answered Uncle Cletis. "Everything wants to be loved."

Walking home from Uncle Celtis' house, Jenny had an idea.

"What if we formed a club to make the lives better for all the animals around and in the shelter? That way, when they passed away, they could go on to next life and not have to come back."

"How could we make them better off?" asked Daniel.

Jenny pointed to Mr. Lee's house. The hunting dogs barely seemed alive, laying on the houses or ground, waiting for the day to pass.

"Take those hunting dogs, if we took them treats and petted them, once a week, they would feel loved. Uncle Celtis said that they could pass over if they felt any kindness and love from humans, even those of a stranger."

Katrina spoke up.

"I ain't messin' with no hunting dogs. Yuck. I mean, I feel sorry for them and all but we could get in trouble. I ain't getting in any trouble." said Katrina firmly.

"You are more of a cat person, aren't you?" asked Jenny.

"Yes, I guess so. My cat, Tinker is just like me, black and beautiful." Katrina laughed.

"Black cats are bad luck, I 'x' them out." said Daniel, he made an 'x' three times with his fingers.

"She is a good cat and not bad luck. That is a stupid superstition." Katrina responded as a cat hissing and spatting. Jenny was quiet. She realized that she cared far more for animals than her friends. She sighed as they passed the Lee place. Katrina sensed her sadness and offered a suggestion.

"I could go by the shelter on Sundays. Uncle Celtis would let me in. He is sweeping up then. I could brush the cats and pet them."

Daniel added, "Yeah, I will go with her and give the dogs some treats, but I don't know about the Lee place. That old man is mean."

Jenny smiled. They reached her house and went in the back yard. Linda was training Maratee and Mary Beth was copying her the best she could, with Tater. The large dog was clumsy and mostly just pulled Mary Beth around but she was up using her legs.

"Hey guys, want to be in a club?" asked Jenny.

Linda put her hands on her hips and asked "What kind of club?"

"Ugly white people club, and you can be the leader." said Katrina matching Linda's posture, hands on the hips.

"Chill." Daniel said.

"The Henry Bergh Society", said Jenny, "a club completely devoted to the dogs and cats in our neighborhood and helping out at the animal shelter.

"Not interested." said Linda.

"Why not?" asked Jenny.

"I want to be in the club." said Mary Beth, at the same time.

"Look, I have a pure bred dog and it is just mix breeds that bite people that go to the pound." Maratee barked at Jenny, as if on cue.

"Not true, Uncle Celtis, had a poodle last week. She was just too old and started wetting the floor during her sleep. So the owner turned her into the pound. A lot of people lose their jobs and can't afford pet food." said Katrina.

"That's awful, said Linda. She knelt down and petted Maratee. "I could never do that." She thought for a moment and smiled, "I will be in your club."

"Great, let's have our first meeting." said Mary Beth. To raise money, they would offer to wash and walk dogs on Saturdays. Katrina would bring a brush to the pound on second Saturdays for the cats. Daniel would accompany her and walk the impounded dogs. Linda and Mary Beth would head up public information. She would make posters on spaying and neutering their dogs. Jenny would offer food and water services for people having problems caring for their dogs.

It became routine for the club to meet up at Uncle Celtis' special place. Linda met with Jenny, Daniel and Katrina after school the next Monday. Mary Beth wanted to go but was fearful of leaving her wheelchair behind to walk up the dirt road.

Cletis greeted them.

"New burial ground over on the left right past that Magnolia tree. In the back of my car are some statues, flowers and a few Gardenia bushes. Care to do some landscaping?"

"Sure." chimed Jenny and Katrina. They went down and examined the plot of land. Linda hung back a bit.

"You mean you actually buried animals there today?" she asked Uncle Cletis.

"Yep, sad but true. I treat the remains with great respect." Linda watched as they unloaded the car and began taking the items over to the plot of land. Daniel and Katrina lifted a ornate iron chair and placed it at the edge of the plot.

"No." said Linda. "The chair needs to be in-between the two Gardenia bushes. Like this."

Linda immediately took over and began placing the flowers, bushes and statues. All followed in on Linda's directions as they were clueless as to where things should be placed. She finished by placed chimes in a tree branch beside a delicate figurine of a cat.

"Seems like someone has a flair for decorating and landscaping", said Uncle Celtis.

CHAPTER NINE

The Henry Bergh Society was off to a great start. Jenny, Linda Kaye and Mary Beth began to make posters for the club. They needed two kinds of posters: those that discouraged people from dropping their pet off at the pound and even more that told of their dog washing and walking services. They had found a ton of magazines behind the library in recycle bin.

"Prince was put down for jumping the fence. Everyone deserves a second chance!' How is that for a poster title?" asked Jenny.

"Great," said Linda Kaye. "Here is a sad looking dog photo."

Mary Beth colored in the letters which read, 'Dog Wash $10. Walk and Wash $20.

The other signs read 'A Tired Dog is A Good Dog' 'Have your Pets Fixed."

Time had passed by. It was almost seven and the dishes were in the sink, the floor needed to be swept and covered with cut up paper from magazines. The dogs were outside, barking. Their school books were all over the couch. They didn't even hear the car pull up.

Ms. Vivian walked through the front door and surveyed the mess. She put her hands on her hips.

"I want the art supplies up and this place clean in twenty minutes. I only have time for a bath before my next shift at work." Ms. Vivian worked sometimes fourteen hours a day and the house needed to be run like a well-oiled machine. Linda Kaye and Jennifer began to move but Mary Beth just sat on the floor coloring.

"I need everyone to start following directions" Ms. Vivian had not resorted to the paddle but tonight was as good of night as any. "Linda Kaye, get the paddle." said Ms. Vivian.

The girls looked up and jumped as if they had seen a spider. Mary Beth continued to color. Jenny and Linda Kaye picked up paper by the hand full and threw it in the trash can.

"Mary Beth, straighten our school books." whispered Jenny.

Mary Beth dumped more crayons on the floor. Linda Kaye had put the paddle on the table and began doing the dishes as Jenny let the dogs in and got them their food.

"Linda Kaye, I said bring me the paddle." Ms. Vivian was like a statue.

Linda Kaye obeyed and Jenny began cleaning up for her sister.

"Jennifer, leave the crayons be. Your sister will pick them up, now." Mary Beth ignored Ms. Vivian.

"Please don't spank her." pleaded Jenny.

Ms. Vivian moved over Mary Beth and began a count down. The dogs could sense the tension. They came over and watched along with Jennifer. Linda Kaye was finishing the dishes.

Ms. Vivian reached over and took Mary Beth by the arm and lifted her. Mary Beth resisted, being dead weight.

"Stand up."

"No."

Smack.

Linda Kaye breathed a sigh of relief. She could tell by the sound that it was not a very hard smack. She had her share of those.

Mary Beth began to cry, really cry.

"My mother is dead, dead." She hugged Ms. Vivian and cried deeply in her large figure. Ms. Vivian hugged her tightly. She sat down on the couch with her. Jenny and Linda Kaye stared.

"You two get busy. Hamburger is in the refrigerator, get busy. Make sure we have a salad. I'm watching my figure. I want to eat with this place clean in twenty five minutes."

"She has never cried." said Jenny. "I just realized that."

As, Jenny swept and cleaned the table, Linda Kaye browned the hamburger. Mary Beth cried and told Ms. Vivian about the accident, what she remembered and how sad she had been. Tater and Maratee laid perfectly still looking on with concern.

****

It was the Saturday of Halloween. The Henry Bergh Club had only met once this weekend. Nick was grounded for fighting. Daniel was grounded for helping Nick. So it was just the girls. All of them wanted to wrap up early to take Mary Beth trick or treating. She had decided to be just a skeleton this year as Ms. Vivian had bought her costume from the sale rack at the K-Mart. Not many people had turned in animals or adopted animals. Either way, it had been slow.

A small Hispanic boy with a thin waste, an over-sized wrestling T-shirt had been walking around in the parking lot. He kept looking at the girls.

"Do you know him?", asked Linda Kaye.

"He's in my Art class." said Mary. "He sticks to himself and never gets in trouble."

"I have seen him in the cafeteria." said Jennifer.

"Hey!" yelled Katrina.

He waved and stuffed his hands in his jean pockets and walked over.

"My name is Felipe. I live over near Nelson's blueberry farm. It is closed now. But I am here with my sisters. My parents are looking for work north of here."

"We help animals." said Mary Beth.

"I know, the whole school talks about the Henry Bergh Club. It is nice what you do." said Felipe.

"How do you say 'big dog' in Spanish?" asked Jennifer.

"el perro grande" answered Felipe He looked down and looked at the shelter.

"Listen, I don't know if you can help me." said Felipe "My dog Sookie was hit by a car."

"Oh no." said the girls together.

"Did he live?" asked Jennifer.

"No, she is in a ditch. It happened yesterday. My sisters won't help

61

me. Girls do not like things like that. I don't want to leave her there. I want to bury her.

The girls looked at each other for an answer.

A lady at the shelter came out to lock the door. She wore the county's tan uniform.

"You kids can go home now. We are closing. You need a ride from your Uncle Cletis, Katrina?

"I need to talk to him for a second!" yelled Katrina.

"You need to hurry." said the woman.

Katrina ran inside the building.

Jennifer, Mary Beth, Linda Kaye began cleaning up. They stacked the signs and Jennifer counted the donations. Felipe helped Mary Beth dump the dog wash tub and put it and the shampoo in a large garbage bag. He kept looking back at the building.

Katrina came running out.

"Uncle Cletis is gonna help you! He said for all of us to meet him around back."

Excited the girls grabbed the signs and bag and went around bag of the building. Uncle Cletis, slowly emerged from the building, hot and tired.

"So you lost your dog to a car, young man?" asked Cletis.

Felipe nodded.

"I know that hurts, how long was she your dog?"

"Four Years. She had puppies twice but we gave them away, except one. I keep the puppy in the house."

"Was she a good momma?"

"The best." said Felipe smiling. It was the first time he had smiled that day.

They all piled in the old Pontiac. Cletis cranked her up. Katrina and Felipe rode shot gun (up front) and the rest of the girls were in the back. It was a twenty minute ride out to Nelson's.

"She is up in that ditch." said Felipe.

Cletis pulled on the side of the road.

He and Felipe got out and walked over. Felipe hung his head and Uncle Cletis put a hand on his shoulder.

"I want to see what kind of dog she was." said Mary Beth, trying to get out.

"No, stay with us." said Jennifer firmly.

In a few minutes, Uncle Cletis came back.

"Jenny, I need your help." Jenny got out of the car and gulped. She did not want to see Sookie but did as Uncle Cletis asked.

The dog was on the shoulder of the road, the life had been knocked out of her. There was no blood. She looked as if she might be sleeping.

"Hold the bag, Jenny. Felipe and I are going to lift her up." Uncle Cletis said.

Jenny looked up and saw the dog, part lab, part terrier wagging it's tail beside Felipe. She gasped.

"You see her don't you, Jenny?" asked Uncle Cletis.

"Yes." Jenny whispered. The dog went toward Jenny and disappeared.

"Felipe, don't be sad. You will see her again." said Jenny smiling.

Uncle Cletis closed the bag and picked up the bag. They walked back to the car and put Sookie in the trunk.

They drove in silence.

"What kind of dog was she?" asked Mary Beth.

"I am not sure." answered Felipe.

"Part lab and a smaller dog. Maybe a terrier." said Jenny.

They sat in silence around Highway sixty four. Jennifer spotted the Dollar Store up ahead.

"Stop, Uncle Cletis." she said.

The three in the backseat piled out, Katrina joined them. In a few minutes, they come running back, smiling with a bag in Mary Beth's hands. As they started back on the highway, Cletis noticed that Felipe was looking down.

"Katrina, Felipe here wants to know where we are going to bury Sookie. Why don't you tell him." asked Cletis.

"My Uncle Cletis is guard of the mystical realm. He has fifty acres up the road about five miles from the shelter and only a mile from our school. You got to know the back roads. He buries the unwanted pets up there in the most beautiful place you ever seen. We all go to yard sales and find little ceramic dogs and cats and decorate his gardens. Uncle

Cletis has every kind of flower bush you can think of from Azaleas to Gardenias. Right now, the leaves are turning yellow and it is still the most beautiful place you ever saw."

"Tell him the rest," said Jennifer.

"Well, no one believes this but Uncle Cletis says the spirits of the animals come out every full moon. They are waiting for their loved ones to die so they can go up to heaven with them."

Felipe made a cross sign and said "Santa Maria!"

They soon arrived at Uncle Cletis' pet cemetery. Felipe got out and looked at all the animal statues, listened to the wind chimes. It was cool but not cold.

"This place is beautiful." said Felipe.

"It is the most beautiful boneyard in the county." bragged Katrina.

"Grab a shovel, young man." said Cletis. "Let's take Sookie on her last walk."

"We used to go everywhere together." Felipe tried to hold back the tears.

"No need to cry, son. You will see her again. Did you love her, feed her, pet her?" asked Uncle Cletis.

"Yes, of course. She was our guard dog. My father built her a nice doghouse." answered Felipe.

"Then she will be there when you die, even if you are a hundred, she will be there, wagging her tail." said Cletis.

They both dug. The girls watched the sunset. Jennifer did a little raking.

"Girls, it's time for the service."

All gathered round as Uncle Cletis said a prayer. Mary Beth began to cry along with Felipe. Even Linda Kaye spilled a tear.

She opened the bag and handed Felipe the dollar store bag. Felipe pulled out a resin dog with orange and black spots on white with a Welcome sign in its mouth. Also, there was a plastic flower, a white rose.

"Good-bye Sookie. I will take care of your puppy." said Felipe. He placed the little dog and flower on the grave.

"It's getting late, time for trick or treat." Uncle Cletis said.

"Want to go with us, Felipe." Mary Beth asked.

"No, my sisters are going to be mad enough. They are preparing for Dias de los Muertos (Day of the Dead)."

"What is Dis de los M…" asked Katrina.

"We set a big table. My sister have made special breads and Tamales. We also fry chicken. These foods are eaten at this time of year and also placed on altars as offerings for the spirits who, it is believed, consume the taste of the foods. We have dolls on the mantle that my grandmother had. We leave empty plates at the table for our ancestors."

"I will ask my sisters if you can come but it is a family holiday. It is not, what is the word, "light" like Halloween.

They drove all the way back to Nelson's and it was dark. Cletis pulled in front of the small house. He and Felipe went past Sookie's dog house and entered the dwelling.

A few minutes later, Felipe came running out of the house.

"I can go trick or treating!"

Cletis and Felipe's father talked on the porch. He and Felipe's mother had just got in from Edenton.

"Felipe, call me." said his father. "I will come pick you up at the Brown house."

The kids were so loud on the way to Ms. Vivian's, that Uncle Cletis had to yell for them to quiet down. It was Halloween and Day of the Dead and everyone was happy.

CHAPTER TEN

November. Katrina had listened to her uncle and how the animals need love to pass over and not have to be reborn. Uncle Cletis had loaned her a large dog carrier and she brought home three kittens and hid the crate in her bedroom. She would keep them until she could find them a home.

While eating a fried fish dinner with collards and fried potatoes, her mother, Dee Dee, her father, Marcel and two younger brothers heard a crash in Katrina's room.

"Pass the hot sauce," said Marcel. As Dee Dee got him the bottle, she heard another noise.

"What's that noise? Is it that cat of yours, Katrina?"

"No." said Katrina, mostly to the peas in her plate.

"Get the gun, if that Antwoine is trying to sneak back in because his daddy's beating him again..."

said Marcel.

"It's not Antwoine, it's cats, three cats." said Katrina, looking at her plate. Dee Dee, a medium sized woman with a red dress and an apron, put her hands on her hips.

"I cannot believe this."

Both parents stared at Katrina in disbelief. The boys giggled until Marcell stared at the boys and they resumed eating.

"You brought another pet, no, not one pet but three pets in this house without asking or saying a word?" asked Dee Dee.

"I am not keeping them. I am a foster. I joined this club with some new friends at school and we are going to help out animals. We wash dogs for money and give information to people turning their animals into the pound. Uncle Cletis..."

"I knew that crazy brother of yours was involved when I heard the word 'cat'. He's crazy. Up there burying them animals in gardens like they were people."

"He lost his wife. His animals are his friends, Marcel."

"Dee Dee, he walked his hound dog every day for ten years. The dog only lived seven years. The leash was dragging the ground."

"He'd never hurt our kids."

"I didn't say he'd hurt them, we have three cats up in here, no four with Tinker, and you know how I hate cats."

Katrina ran to her room, crying and shut the door.

Her daddy yelled, "If you gonna be a foster, bring home a Pit bull, something with some teeth to keep people out of our yard."

This was a sore subject between Katrina's parents. They argued about whether Uncle Cletis was right in the head and forgot about the cats for a while.

The next day, Katrina was told to find homes for the three cats within a month, and then, maybe they would consider letting her foster one animal at a time.

And there was even one more silver lining, a pitbull dog would find a home. To Marcel, it woud be a useful guard dog but would become the family's beloved baby. It was to be a long journey for the small brown pit bull with white paws and a white snout.

The Washingtons had never had a dog. Katrina two younger brothers were filled with joy at the very mention of getting a pup.

Uncle Cletis had watched over this young dog as he was rescued from a dog fighting ring over in the next county. Due to his young age and lack of aggression, the young dog had ribs showing and a large chain for a collar. He could barely lift his head. He was "hand shy" as Uncle Cletis said to Katrina.

"Did he have to fight other dogs, Uncle Cletis?" asked Katrina.

"Oh no. He was a puppy, has not known the company of people or dogs. Those dogs that had to fight would not make good pets with young children. They need a grown-up that understand what they have been through and the precautions they should take. This little fellow is shy because he has been off to himself his whole life. Make sure you tell LaMichael and Greg not to run up on him. Treat him like a baby chick, pet him a lot and make sure h has some play things."

Katrina went to pet the dog and he cowered in a corner and yelped a high pitch scream. Katrina yanked her hand back in shock while the dog, tale tucked, withered away from her.

"Try again. He won't bite."

She reached over and ignored the dog's cries and began to pet him. Soon the dog turned and the tale came out some and he responded to Katrina's soft touch with a wag and then, a lick.

"That's right. The dog was a year old, not a puppy so Katrina could not bundle him up in her arms and give him the love he needed.

"What do we call him?"

"I named him 'Bruno' which means brown. But you folks come up with a name."

Katrina had Mary Beth make her a 'free kitten' sign and though they were full grown cats, they found homes. Miracles do happen. As people would come up to Katrina's "Free Cats" stand, Katrina had prepared instruction for every interested person.

"Take them over to Craven County and have them fixed so they won't be having kittens. They have a special for cats, "Find 'em and Fix 'em" program where the surgery is discounted". Katrina gave flyers to the new owners. "If things don't work out, bring them back." she would say.

LaMichael and Greg said together, "No, we want a dog!"

The new cat owners would just laugh. Katrina was very professional in her interview.

"Have you ever owned a cat before?"

"Cats are meat eaters and have to have food and water available for them. Keep them inside for at least three days so they will know their home. Put them out if you want them to keep pest out of the yard but only if they had the surgery or you will get more kittens. Fixing them will keep them home."

Jenny, Mary Beth and Linda Kaye were present for the cat-a-thon. It was a unseasonably warm day in November. Gray clouds and a cool breeze made the three girls ware sweaters. They gave a bag of cat chow, a litter box and one bag of litter with each cat. "Here are some coupons for flea protection." Even the manager of the local pet store supported The Henry Bergh Club.

Ms. Vivian had helped the kids with the food, litter boxes, and leashes for dog. She explained to her employer at the convenience store that these items could be labeled as "gifts" when tax time rolled around.

Finally, with the last cat gone, Katrina could bring Bruno home. He had grown into a friendly dog, eager to play with boundless energy, just like the boys. Katrina walked through the door with the dog on a leash. She had given him a bath and put a big red ribbon around his neck.

"Here he is everybody."

The boys ran over to the dog and Katrina held up her hand

"Stop! Don't ever run up on a dog like that! Come up slowly. Hold out your hand to see if the dog is friendly."

"He better be be friendly, well not too friendly. He could bite that Antwoine." said Marcel.

"I am sure Cletis would not send some dog over here that have been in some kind of dog fighting ring. Would he? Katrina?"

"This dog is friendly, Mama. I was just telling the boys so they would not get bit by another dog."

The boys got on their knees and began petting him. There was a knock on the door. It was Uncle Cletis.

"Anyone need a fifty pound bag of dog chow?"

Marcel went and got the bag and exchanged pleasantries with his brother in law.

"The food will go in the wash room where he can sleep. Thank you for the food Cletis. We can let Tinker sleep with Katrina."

They all sat in a circle in the living room watching the boys wrestle with the dog.

"Yelp!"

The dog hid under Katrina's legs.

"I know who's dog he really is." said Dee Dee.

"Y'all too rough. Play nice with him."

Greg rolled on his back and the dog came out and licked his face.

"See any more ghost dogs and cats?" asked Marcel.

"Marcel." said Dee Dee with clinched teeth.

Uncle Cletis just laughed.

"Not until the full moon, you want to go out to the cemetery with me after dark, Marcel. You may see a ghost or two."

"We go to the cemetery on Sundays during the day. O.K. Bedtime boys." said Marcel.

"Awe, we have not named the dog yet."

"I have been calling him Bruno, for his color." said Uncle Cletis.

"Let's call him Donatello!" said LaMichael.

"Yeah." agreed Greg.

"They are Ninja Turtle fans." explained Dee Dee.

"I like Bruno, that is a tough name." said Marcel.

"Me too." said Katrina.

All looked toward Dee Dee.

"Don't expect me to break this tie. I bet his name is going 'Trouble'. I don't know."

Dee Dee got down on one knee.

The dog wiggled over to her. She petted him.

"I once had a pony that had a white face and chest like this, let's name him 'Blaze'."

"We like Bruno better." said Marcel.

"Bruno, it is." she said, with a sigh.

Later, that evening all listened to the whimpering dog as they laid in bed. Marcel and Dee Dee stared at the ceiling.

"What have we done." said Marcel.

"It will be fine, he just has to adjust." answered Dee Dee.

"Hush that dog up, Katrina." yelled Marcel.

Katrina tip toed to the wash room and opened the door.

"He said hush you up, he did not say how."

The dog with all his clumsy might climbed it's way unto the bed. The house was quiet once again.

CHAPTER ELEVEN

It was a quiet Sunday after Thanksgiving break, and Washington, North Carolina was having a cold snap. It was unusual for the area to get snow flurries and freezing temperatures in the lower south east of the country. The yards were still covered with leaves. A white dust covered them and many scampered to ready their yards for more unseasonable weather.

Mary Beth had a soft ball and was playing with Tater and Maratee. She would bounce the ball on the floor and watch the dogs scramble for it. Tater held it proudly in her mouth.

"Good girl, now fetch it here." said Mary Beth. Tater would run into another room, carrying the ball with pride in her mouth. She would look around to make sure the chase was still on.

Mary Beth chased her. She took the ball out of her mouth.

"Watch, Tater."

She threw the ball to Maratee. The poodle pranced over and retrieved the ball, brought it back and laid it at Mary Beth's feet. Before she could pick it up, Tater had it in her mouth and ran under the kitchen table. Hitting her head on a chair, Tater let go the ball and Mary Beth had to reach under the sink to get it.

Jenny kept watch by the window of her bedroom. She kept an eye out for Ms. Vivian who would restrict both her and her sister if Tater was caught 'rough housing' in the house. She was also reading her tablet.

Daniel tapped on the window and Jenny jumped.

"You scared me!" she said. He came around to the front door and entered. Picking up the ball, he tossed it to Tater who scrambled to get it. Maratee just sat and whined.

"What are you doing?" asked Daniel, entering Jenny's room.

"Reading." She placed the book down. Daniel looked at the title.

"'Out of the Darkness. The Story of Mary Ellen Wilson.' What is that about?"

"Remember my report about Henry Bergh, the man who found the A.S.P.C.A?"

"The whole school remembers the day Katrina knocked Zeb on his ass! What does A.S... whatever that stand for again?"

Jenny rolled her eyes and shook her head.

"American Society for the Prevention of Cruelty to Animals. Any ways, there was this girl named Mary Wilson. She was kept in a closet and beaten everyday by her foster parents. They would not even buy her shoes for the winter."

"What, did they beat their pets, too?" Daniel laid casually back on the bed, propping his head up with his hands.

"No. The police could not do anything because it was a family matter. There were no child abuse laws in the 1870's. So this lady wrote Henry Bergh and he took her out of the home. He said that she was an animal too, as all humans are. Later, he and his lawyer friend made the Society for the prevention of cruelty to children."

"I wish I could call the A.S.P.C.C. on my dad then." said Daniel. "I am grounded again."

"How did you get over here?" asked Mary Beth.

"He has to work until six. They are always busy on Saturdays."

Suddenly, Tater jumped in the middle of the bed, knocking the book on the floor. She had the ball in her mouth.

"Tater!" Mary Beth ran in and joined the dog on the bed, hugging her. Maratee followed. It was a free for all. Daniel, Jennifer and Mary Beth wrestled with the huge dog. Linda Kaye busted into the house.

"Guess what?" She yelled.

They all sat up and looked at her.

"Nick ran away and he is up at the Porter house. He sent a message to bring him food and stuff." She held out her cell phone for all to see.

"The Porter house? It is too cold." said Jenny. She would make any excuse not to go up there. It was not the weather but the idea of the old house sent chills to her bones.

"Come on guys, you gotta help me. He's my boyfriend!" Linda went into the bathroom and began making up her face. She brushed her hair. "We can stop my the store. I got cash. I figure peanut butter sandwiches and a large soda."

Wrapped up with wool scarfs, toboggans, both dogs on a leash and two layers of coats, the four left the house and headed toward the path. Jenny held on to Tater with a tight grip. He was pulling a bit. Mary Beth leaned on Tater's back. Maratee followed along, daintily jumping each log and vine.

"Why did he run away?" asked Daniel.

"His mom said I was a bad influence." answered Linda Kaye.

"You probably are." joked Daniel back.

"If anything, he is a bad influence on you." said Jenny. She looked up and saw the house. The woods were so thick, it was necessary to be close to even see it. Most of the vines were dead. It seemed huge. The walls seemed to be reaching out to her. Jenny remembered her babysitter, her injuries, the little girl in white and most of all, how angry her parents were. Fear grasped Jenny and it felt like ice water was in her veins. The gray wood had a white paint chips peeling. Most of the large windows were busted out. Smoke rose out of the chimney. The house was somehow alive.

Daniel cautiously pushed on the front door. It creaked.

"Mary Beth, watch your step on this porch. I see some holes and it could fall through." said Jenny.

Nick yanked open the door and yelled "Boo!!" Dressed in jeans and two hooded sweat shirts, he seemed satisfied that he had scared them. Younger than the rest, Mary Beth hung back and stared at her feet. She was scared to death. Tater barked, as well as Maratee.

All screamed and Daniel seemed to be the loudest.

"You sound like a little girl." said Nick to Daniel.

He touched Linda's face and kissed her on the lips.

"Thanks. Come into my house." Nick made a grand gesture of

welcome with his arms. He had enough sense to have a flannel sleeping bag and a knapsack full of flannel shirts. There was a fire in the fireplace. Nick plopped down on his sleeping bag and took the peanut butter and bread out. He pulled a large knife out of his pocket. Mary Beth stayed closely behind Jenny. Jenny was not attracted to Nick at all and looked around at what had been a beautiful Victorian mansion. She could not imagine such wealth, but most of all, abandoning the house like a discarded travel trailer. The dogs began exploring the inside of the empty house with their noses. There was nothing but dust, grime and dirt on the walls and floor. Part of the house had been spared, part was gone, weeds and vines had taken over.

"This is dangerous. You could burn the house down with that fireplace." said Jenny.

"So." said Nick. "It is mostly gone anyways. Call 911 if you are really worried." Nick had a teasing grin.

"I might." countered Jenny.

"You do and I will beat your ..." started Nick. He was stopped by a thump from the floor above them. "It is haunted for sure." said Nick. Munching on his peanut butter sandwich, he pulls a Ouija board out of his sleeping bag. It was a yellowish board with letters, numbers and the words 'yes' and 'no'.

"Check it out." said Nick.

"Snap, I have never done this. Let's talk to the dead!." said Daniel.

Jenny blurted out, "My mother would not allow a Ouija board in the house! She said, 'It opens the door for demons!'"

Everyone looked at her with disapproval. Jenny changed her frame of mind to suit her friends.

"I'm cool, but Mary Beth is a little scared." said Jenny.

"No, I'm not." Mary went down on her knees, and rubbed her hand on the board.

"She will be okay." said Linda Kaye. They all sat in a circle. Linda Kaye touched one side of the pointer and Daniel took the other.

"Are there any ghosts here?" asked Linda. She had her armed cupped through Nick's arm. Slowly the pointer began to move.

"You are moving it." yelled Jenny.

Nick laughed. Each took turns. The pointer moved but no one could trust the other. Mostly, the ghost hunting game just broke down into laughter.

"I am going to find Tater and Maratee. Then we have to get home or we will be in trouble." said Jenny.

She got up and walked into the other room. Folding her arms across her chest, she went into what might have been the kitchen. Cabinets doors dangled open. She whistled looking for the dogs. Maratee came running up to Jenny. Tater appeared at the top of the stairs barking.

"Tater, come." said Jenny, patting her knees. The dog turned and ran into a room.

"Tater, now!" yelled Jenny. She gingerly put one foot on the bottom stair step. It creaked but seemed firm. She carefully went up the stairs, testing each step. Maratee walked beside of her.

"Tater." she whispered. She could hear his barks but when she reached the first room, the door slowly moved. She pushed it open. The dog's bark seemed far away. Not wanting to enter, she went to the next room. The door was off the hinge. Maratee perked up her ears and began to bark. Jenny looked inside. Nothing. Tater came out off the last room and Jenny sighed. She was shaking. She picked up the leash and glanced back into the room. Glancing out the window toward the woods, Jenny froze with fear. A small blonde haired girl in white night gown stared at her from the woods. Within a second, the girl was behind Jenny and her lips were close enough to touch Jenny's ear.

"I want my dolly." As if in a dream, Jenny found herself in the house as it was in 1820. The wall paper had delicate roses. There was a huge family celebrating Christmas. Relatives were coming in. The tree was in the center of the room and tiny candles were lit on the tips of the branches.

Then, the family disappeared. The tree was by itself and the little girl went to light one of the candles. It was very late at night. Jenny watched. The dogs paced with a nervous gate and circled Jenny in an unnatural way. Jenny felt heat. Fire surrounded her. She ran down the stairs toward her laughing friends.

With a face as white as paper ashes, Jenny yelled, "I am out of here." She went through the door with the dogs on her heal. Mary Beth and Daniel ran after her. Nick and Linda Kaye stood at the door and laughed.

"Chicken!" Nick yelled.

Jenny stumbled on a vine and went face down with a thud. Tater licked her face. Mary Beth took one side and Daniel took another, lifting Jenny to her feet. She looked over her shoulder to the mansion. Jenny gasped. The little girl in the white gown was in a upstairs window looking down at her.

"Are you okay?" asked Mary Beth. Daniel had his arms folded up and flapping imitating a chicken. He turned in circles and laughed. "Chicken!"

"Do you see her? asked Jenny. "The girl in the window, do you see her?"

"I don't see anyone but Nick and Linda Kaye. Can't we just go home?" whined Mary Beth.

"I only see one girl". said Nick. He grabbed Linda around the waist and gave her a long kiss. The others just stared at them, except for Jenny. Her eyes were trained on the house. The window was empty. All, except Nick, headed home.

Jenny never mentioned her vision or the Christmas tree burning to the others. Nick eventually went home. The Porter house was abandoned again. It was rumored that it would be completely torn down next summer and most of the adults sighed with relief. The house had been such a temptation for their children, it was just plain dangerous.

CHAPTER TWELVE

The next day Katrina could not over to Jenny and Linda Kaye's house. She was in enough trouble. Her mother discovered that the Bruno had been sleeping with her at night and Marcel built a dog house for Bruno outside. The young dog paced back and forth stopping only to bark at the house.

"That dog is barking all the time." said Marcel. "SOME ONE SHUT THAT DOG UP!"

"He's bored." said Katrina, answered in a loud tone.

"Linda Kaye and Jenny make sure their dogs are walked every day and their behavior is better. It lets off some energy.

"If the boys play with him, he runs off." said Dee Dee.

"We need a fenced in backyard like Jenny." said Katrina.

Marcel shook his head and put his hand on his hips. He walked in the laundry room. Dee Dee and Katrina were doing laundry together.

"I just spent a hundred on the dog house, line and the bucket. Now we need a fence?"

"The boys could play ball with him that way."

Marcel just sighed and looked at his wife.

"I'll tell you what, Katrina," said Dee Dee, "you and I will take him for a walk since you helped me with the laundry."

Katrina beamed. "Great."

They clipped the leash onto the collar and the dog bounded toward the back door. The dog went in a zig zag motion through the house. They opened the front door and the Bruno was fine, sniffing the area. It was not until he got out on the street that the problem occurred. Bruno pulled and Dee Dee nearly fell down.

Dragging them to the street, Dee Dee wondered how other people walked their dogs. Was this normal? She felt nervous.

They had not gone far. Katrina thought for a moment. What had Linda Kaye done with Tater and Maratee before walking them? Katrina took the dog from her mother and began walking back toward her own house. A nosy neighbor appeared on her porch. Her name was Hattie May.

"What are you doing?" Dee Dee asked.

A boy appeared on the porch beside Hattie May and another joined him. "That's a Pitt bull! He will kill you as fast as he looks at you!" said the large woman to the boys.

Katrina started to yell back but her mother stopped her.

"Let's just get on by them." said Dee Dee. She smiled and waved. 'What would the neighbors say if she could not control the dog and her daughter?' she thought.

And things went downward from there. In the blink of an eye, what should have been a peaceful walk turned into a dangerous nightmare.

A dog came running toward Dee Dee and Katrina. To the humans, it was just a small Chihuahua but to Bruno, it was a threat to his masters. Bruno went into a full pull. The neighbor screamed. People came out on their porches. Bruno attached the dog. There was a huge scuffle. Mr. Jenkins who owned the little dog came running out of his house screaming "General! General!"

Dee Dee was dragged into the street and Katrina took hold of Bruno's collar off of the small dog. She screamed "NO" over and over.

It seemed to last an hour but it was only a few seconds. General got out from under Bruno and was just wet from slobber. He ran to his master who was yelling at Dee Dee. She managed to get to her feet and looked down at her scrapped knees, blotting them with a tissue.

"I am fine, thank you, Mr. Jenkins.!"

The woman across the street was saying, "I saw the whole thing. I'm calling the police." Katrina began to cry while helping her mother.

Marcel came out of his house with the two boys. He took control of Bruno who was still pulling.

"You let 'General' go wherever he wants to go, so you are the one who put him at risk!" said Marcel to the man.

They had not gone far. Katrina thought for a moment.

"What are you doing?" asked Dee Dee

"Calling Jenny's house." said Katrina.

"The white girl who goes to dog shows?"

The police car pulled up and a large man got out of the car. He said something into the communication device on his shoulder and walked up to the group of chattering women and yelling men.

The neighbor came out and went right up to the police officer.

"They got a Pitt Bull. That dog will kill you as soon as the looks at you."

"That's not true. This was our first walk. Mr Jenkin's dog ran toward us into the street."

"Let me see the little dog and then let me see the Pitt Bull." said the officer. He was examining General by picking him up and looking him over for injuries. The little dog nipped at the officer.

"Ouch! It's nothing but with his temperament, Mr. Jenkins, you shouldn't let him run free. A little girl could pick him up and get bit."

The officer took Bruno by his collar and walked around the squad car. He petted the dog and Bruno wagged his tail. He called into the station for animal control.

Linda Kaye and Jenny pulled up on their bikes. Linda had brought a slip leash that she used for dog shows. She had several.

"WE GOT YOUR 911", Linda Kaye yelled.

"We can't have a dog like that in our neighborhood!" Hattie May said. She put her hands on her hips. Her bright blue house dress shined in the sun.

"A dog like what?" said Linda Kaye in a strong assertive manner.

"Who you?" said Hattie May.

"Pit Bulls have a bad rap. They were once called "The Nanny Dogs" because of their protective nature to their owners. If the little dog was charging toward Bruno, he presumed it was a threat but only dominated the dog as there are clearly no bite marks. I see no blood. Bruno could of killed a dog of this size within seconds. The little dog submitted to Bruno, so Bruno could not hurt it."

"Who you?" said Hattie May again.

"I agree with the young lady." said the officer. "No harm, no fowl." He petted Bruno and saw no signs of aggression. "And Mr. Jenkins, you may not want 'General' to run free anymore. He could be hit by a car."

"You still got to get rid of that dog!" Nosy Hattie May was not giving up.

Greg looked up at his father and asked, "Are we gonna have to get rid of Bruno?"

Marcel looked down at his son and then turned in her direction to the woman who stood fast we her hands on her hips.

"Bruno is a member of the family now. We do not just dump members of the family when there are problems. We work them out." He voice was firm and loud.

"Marcel, please. Let's fence in the back yard so the boys can play with the dogs."

Linda Kaye put the training collar on Bruno.

"Let's finish the walk, Katrina. I'd like General to join us, if that is alright with Mr. Jenkins. I have an extra leash."

"Whaaat?" said Dee Dee.

Hattie May yelled, "George Jenkins, you dare let General get ate by that dog."

The police man handed Linda Kaye 'General'. He said "you seem to know dogs young lady, Mr. Jenkins?" He nodded toward the neighbor.

Uncle Cletis came pulling up in his white county van.

"It is alright, I know this family and the girls." Uncle Cletis said to the officer.

"It will be alright." George said, embarrassed that General had nipped an officer.

"Let's meet proper." Linda Kaye picked up the little dog and put it's butt in Bruno's face and allowed him to sniff. She set the small dog on the ground and firmly said, "Bruno, be nice." She clipped the slip leash on General and said, "care to join us Mr. Jenkins?"

"You sure you know what you are doing?" said Mr. Jenkins.

"Watch." Katrina said. "These are my friends."

Jenny, Linda Kaye and Katrina walked away from the adults, all staring in amazement. The dogs were fine. They turned back after a few minutes and waved at the police man as he left.

"Bruno knew you were nervous, Mom." said Katrina. "He thought you were afraid of that little dog."

"You can have this training collar. You see, you hold the dog at your side, hold it up by his ears. Don't let him pull on it or they will drag you worse. Also, make sure the dog is not too excited before he goes on the walk. Calm him down with a command of your choice."

Dee Dee said, "I'm done walking dogs. You girls can stay for supper if you'd like."

Marcel walked away with his sons. "I am building in a fenced in backyard and if you boys throw that dog a ball for an hour, that will get him calm."

The Pit bull is one of the most misused breeds. Once known as a nanny dog, the pit bull guarded children with their lives. Extremely loyal, pit bulls are used for fighting, however, depending on how they are raised, Pit Bulls can be a nice pet. The Chihuahua is the the smallest breed. Once bred for royalty in South America, the Chihuahua was killed and buried with his master. Small dogs can become possessive of a person or objects and need to be taught boundaries.

CHAPTER THIRTEEN

Soon the club acted like a well-oiled machine. On Monday afternoons they wouldd protest at the animal shelter where Uncle Cletis worked. The girls were very good at making signs about spaying and neutering the pets. OVER POPULATION IS THE PROBLEM was their most effective sign according to Uncle Cletis. They advertised their washing and walking services on Saturdays at Ms. Vivians' store. This generated a great deal of income which was spent on the cost of cat and dog food for those turning their pets into the shelter because they could no longer afford food. Daniel and Nick road with Uncle Cletis on Sundays to deliver the food. They rode on bikes and carpooled with parents. Most of the customers seemed to be nearby.

It was on a Saturday that Jenny met Regina Whitney, the richest and most miserly woman in town. She was a small woman and had the second largest home on the river. She drove up with her overweight German Shepard.

She rolled one window down for the dog and drove over to the group of kids.

"I only have five dollars but will you wash my Cocoa?" Jenny hesitated and looked at the rest of the group. Katrina shook her head "no", Linda shrugged and Mary Beth blurted out, "of course, we will!"

Daniel quickly added, "First time only, from then on, ten dollars for large dogs."

And so, the nightmare of washing Cocoa began. The whole group showed up to Mrs. Whitney' house the following afternoon. It was a typical 1920's style house with a big rambling porch, swing and a lot of flowers around the house. Slightly cool, but good weather for early December.

Cocoa laid, head down staring at the group. She growled and barked, making the whole group stop in their tracks. The dog lowered her head and continued to growl as the kids set up the large tub and found the water hose.

Mrs. Whitney came to the front door.

"Don't mind Cocoa. She is a German Shepherd and they naturally warn their owners if someone approaches. German Shepherds were used in every war to sleep in the trenches with soldiers, listening for any unwanted enemy. They growl and bark once to let the soldier wake up."

"Can you tell her we are not the Japanese and this isn't World War Two?" asked Jenny. "She won't bite, I promise." insisted Mrs. Whitney.

Nick took the dog by the collar and headed toward the barrel. Cocoa saw what was coming and dropped to the ground, digging her claws in the ground with all her weight. Daniel went over and tried to pick up her back end. Cocoa whined. Jenny and Nick pulled on the collar. The dog would not budge. Jenny talked to the dog in a sweet voice. Cocoa eyed her as if she had lost her mind. All four tried to lift Cocoa to the tub, but her dead weight was too much. Without warning, the water hose with a power nozzle was turned on Cocoa and the whole group.

"I don't have all day!" yelled Linda. "We are only getting five dollars!" Soaked all over, everyone lathered Cocoa from head to all four paws, rinsed her and towel dried the dog who by that time was loving the attention.

"Why is she limping?" asked Jennifer.

"She has bad arthritis and hip dyspepsia. Cocoa was born that way." said Mrs. Whitney. She handed a dollar to each of them and handed Jennifer six, five for the wash and one for a tip.

"Oh, it was the breeder over in Craven County. If dogs are bred over and over again in the same family, physical problems happen, according to the breed. I won't use that breeder again."

"Come on, let's go!" yelled Linda Kaye.

"Yeah, we are wet!" Daniel said.

"Go ahead!" yelled Jennifer.

Mrs. Whitney invited Jennifer in and gave her a cup of hot chocolate. Jennifer looked on the wall. There were pictures of four German Shepherds, all different but definitively the same breed.

"This Cocoa was my first, I won't love any of them the way I loved her. She lost the use of her legs, only at eleven years of age. It killed me to put her down." She pointed to the second picture.

"After my husband passed away, I was so lonely. This Cocoa was so shy. She was scared of everything. The arthritis had started at ten, so I gave her away to a couple who did not mind having to buy all that expensive medication."

"Now, this Cocoa, the one I had before the Cocoa you washed, was a runner. She was a handful. I kept her as long as I could, until she could not walk and I turned her over to the pound. I could not stand to take her to the vet and have her put down. That is why I met your little club, this Cocoa is beginning to limp. If I surrender her to the pound, they will 'put her to sleep' for me. Then, I can go ahead and get Cocoa number five. I know of a breeder in Raleigh that has just had puppies. Only seven hundred for females."

Jennifer could not believe what she was hearing. She looked down at the wet Cocoa and noticed her limp as she turned.

"How can you do this? Why can't you take her to the vet and get some medicine?"

"Oh, it would cost so much and I just love puppies. Do you not love a puppy?"

Jennifer's face turned red and she put the six dollars beside her cup of chocolate.

"You need this money more than I do." At that, she leaped up and ran out of the door, crying. Freezing, she ran all the way home, not wanting to think about dogs ever again.

German Shepherds are known for their police work and military jobs. Their ability to make smell explosives and intelligence make for an excellent working partner. A new breed founded in the 1800s, The German Shepard Dog herded sheep and their multi-layered coats made them ideal for the cold. Despite hip problems they are the second most popular pet and if socialized as pups, they are not dangerous. They are high energy dogs and need lots of exercise. German Shepherd mixes make even better pets, often calmer. Look for a dog with a black snout.

CHAPTER FOURTEEN

The next afternoon, all had stuff to do at home. With the landscaping at Uncle Cletis' burial grounds, sign making and afternoons at the shelter, all were behind on their homework. It was mutually agreed that Tuesday and Wednesday had to be taken off.

On the following Thursday, Jenny brought up a sore subject with the group. The hunting dogs.

"Mr. Lee is crazy, we will get in trouble." insisted Daniel. Katrina agreed.

"I'll take him on!" boasted Nick.

"I guess you like jail, Nick." Daniel countered.

"Listen," said Jenny, "Linda Kaye told me the bread man picks up sandwiches and cakes that won't sell. Ms. Vivian said we could have them. She also says old man Lee goes off every Friday somewhere, like clock-work. He always stops and fills up his car and heads north on 301. We can feed and tend to the dogs on Fridays."

"I am sure I can get Mom to give me the food." said Linda, "I will even tell her why, everyone in town feels sorry for those dogs."

The group parted and agreed to meet on Friday after old man Lee left.

Friday was overcast and chilly. Except for the pines, the leaves had all fallen. The trees naked branches reached up to the sky like the boney fingers of an old woman trying to grasp crab apples from a thorny tree.

School would be out in a week for Christmas and all were excited about getting out for the holidays. It was so hard to concentrate in school.

Friday afternoon finally came and the gang met up near old man Lee's house.

"His car is gone, just like Mom said." said Linda Kaye.

The dogs began barking and wagging their tails. A few cars passed by. They were coon hounds, medium size, white with orange and black spots, their tails drooped, thin and long.

"Oh, their water is horrible said Katrina, "I will find the hose. Keep them on one end while I dump the bucket."

Each grabbed a sandwich from the bag Linda Kaye had gotten from her mother and unwrapped it.

"You think they will like egg salad?" asked Jenny.

"They are so thin, they'd like peanut butter and jelly!" said Nick, as he threw the first one and several dogs ascended on it, almost fighting.

"We have to throw ours all at once so they won't fight!" yelled Jenny over the barks. "One, Two, Three..."

Five sandwiches went in and were gobbled up. After the second set, Jenny instructed everyone to feed through the fence to earn trust.

Katrina shocked everyone. The prissy cat woman walked around with a rake cleaning and petting each dog she passed. "Look at their tails!" said Mary Beth, "they are curled up."

"That means they are happy..." started Jenny.

BAM!

"What you doing messing with my dogs?!" yelled Mr. Lee. He carried a twenty gage shot gun and shot again, over their heads. Wearing overalls and a plaid shirt, Lee had forgotten something and returned home. He eyed the group and lifted the gun to take aim.

BAM!

Needless to say, everyone dropped everything and ran, ran for their lives. But Linda Kaye went down.

Across the road, they all stopped to catch their breath. Leaning over and breathing hard, Jenny said, "that was close. I am sorry, guys."

BAM

All looked to see Zeb Lee pulling the shot gun to the ground and shouting at his uncle.

"They my friends. Uncle Joe." Zeb cried.

"Where's Linda Kaye?" asked Katrina. All raised up and looked around.

"Oh no." cried Mary Beth.

"I'll be shot first." yelled Nick. He ran back across jumping the two ditches and stood face to face with Mr. Lee.

"Shoot me. I don't care. Where's Linda?" said Nick definitely. The rest of the group watched from the other side of the road.

"I caused this, I am going too." said Jenny as she crossed the road to join Nick.

"Y'all crazy." Katrina said as she walked toward the direction of home. She thought about Linda Kaye, wounded, maybe even dead and turned around.

"Old man, if she is hurt, you are in trouble." yelled Katrina.

"Ain't got no business messing..." said Lee.

Jenny interrupted.

"You don't feed them or hunt them. You are mean and everyone knows it. Where is Linda Kaye?"

"Shhh!" yelled Daniel who had joined them.

"I hear crying."

"There she is!" yelled Nick. Linda Kaye had fallen in the tall grass and was terrified. Nick and Daniel helped her to her feet and Jenny looked her over. She had torn her blouse and just scraped a knee but it was not bad.

"That will teach you brats." said Mr. Lee and he spit before he went inside his old house. He pushed Zeb.

"I'm sorry!" Zeb yelled.

"Let's get you home." Nick said to Linda Kaye.

Everyone called it a day. Coming through George Brown's door, Jenny, Linda Kaye and Mary Beth were convinced that they were in very bad trouble. Ms. Vivian was angry, hands on her hips, ready to rip through them like a lawnmower on grass in June, until she saw her daughter.

"I'm sorry, Mama. We were just giving the hunting dogs the sandwiches like we said we were going to do. He shot at us, twice." She cried harder as Ms. Vivian bandaged her knee, in silence.

"It's not that bad, Jenny, Mary Beth, you girls all right?" asked Ms. Vivian. They nodded.

"Call in a pizza, then get ready for bed. I want supper on the table before I get back."

"Where are you going, Mama?"

Holding a phone to her ear and getting her special black purse, Ms. Vivian just said, "grown up business."

"Joe, get the sheriff on the line, Lee shot at my kids for feeding his dogs. I'll meet him over there." She dropped the phone on the couch and turned.

"The club is over. Consider yourselves restricted." Jenny swallowed and pushed back her tears. Mary Beth petted Tater and Maratee curled up beside Linda Kaye, giving her licks as if she knew her master was hurt. And she did. Dogs know.

Nick knocked on the window. Daniel peered inside. Linda opened the door and yelled, "Come around here, Mama's gone."

"Let's see what's going on!" said Daniel. Linda's leg hurt too bad and Mary Beth was terrified of her step mother but Jenny was up and ready to go back.

"Tell us what happened." yelled Linda as they went off into the night.

Edging up along the highway, Daniel and Nick saw the commotion. Three sheriff cars were at the Lee house. The blue lights were flashing. The kids bent slightly and ran along the road until close enough then cut through the cars and then went behind the house. They could hear an argument.

"They were trespassing. Clear and simple." said Lee to a deputy.

"So? There is still daylight and you see children feeding your hounds and the right thing to do is use deadly force?" asked the sheriff in a harsh voice.

Lee began swearing as he saw that he had little to no chance of winning this argument.

"How often do you feed those dogs?" asked Sheriff Wingate.

"Once or twice a week." blurted out Lee.

"You feed dogs once a day, every day, you old coot." yelled Wingate.

"That Brown girl always has been eying my dogs. Tell her to mind her own business." yelled Lee. The deputies began leaving, one by one. The dogs were barking, radio calls could be heard from the two remaining cars.

"We are going to issue you a warning to you and those children. In the meantime, I am impounding those dogs until their weight is up. Do you understand how lucky you are Mr. Lee? If you had killed one of those kids, I would have put you under the jail. Understand?"

Lee knew he had been licked. He shook his head.

"Jackson, go get my cousin and his dog truck, my cousin can feed and house them until they get fit." yelled Wingate.

"Yes, sir. It will take me a couple of hours."

"Just have them out of here by tomorrow morning."

The cars pulled out. The ugliest house on the road was quiet again.

Mrs. Morris sat on her porch. Jenny, Nick and Daniel were standing with her watching the blue lights. Then, Jenny noticed one car still on the side of the road. It was Ms. Vivian's car. They crossed the ditch and went by the pen on tip toes. They peaked into the windows. Mr. Lee had a one bedroom house and he lived mostly in the front room. There were pots and pans hanging from the ceiling and a bed was pushed in the corner. An overhead light was the only illumination.

Ms. Vivian had pulled a small gun from her purse and Mr. Lee was stuttering and shaking his finger at her. He backed up by the end of the bed. Nick, Jenny and Daniel's eyes were wide. They could hear Mr. Lee pleading with Ms. Vivian.

"No one hurts my Linda Kaye. No one. If you ever, and I mean ever, even look at my girl again, I will kill you myself. I won't even bother calling the law."

She aimed the gun. Jennifer gasped and covered her mouth. This could not be happening. It would be the last begging breath for Mr. Lee. Ms. Vivian had a steady hand and a good shot. She pointed the gun at Lee's head and raised it up to the ceiling and hit the nail holding a large black skillet which fell and hit Mr. Lee on the head. He fell back onto the bed. After Ms. Vivian left, then Jenny had to check and see if Mr. Lee was just unconscious.

Entering the house with a quick and silent stride, they ambled (went up slowly) up to Mr. Lee and listened for his breath. It was confirmed when he turned over and punched his pillow. They all ran out the back door with a leap.

Nick yelled at Daniel, "Hey Daniel, don't you think it is cold tonight?"

"It's a little chilly, so what?" yelled Daniel back. He had to get home.

"So the hunting dogs need to come in the house for the night." laughed Nick. And with that, the final act of revenge was played on Mr. Lee. Jenny pulled out her camera phone to cheer the other girls up with picture of dogs sprawled all over the bed and floor as Mr. Lee snored with his mouth open.

"You got your Ipod, Nick?" asked Daniel.

"Always packin' my favorite music. Why?"

"Got a photo app?" The three kids smiled.

It was unknown how the picture of old man Lee sleeping with all his hunting dog circulated around the county and found it's way in the Washington Daily News, but it did. The picture of Lee with his mouth wide open and a coon dog curled around his head became legend.

From then on, Mr. Lee's dog pen was a model dog enclosure for hunting dogs. No more barrels, raised dogs houses with flaps to keep the cold out. Running water from his pump filled a baby pool which was always full and clean. In fact Sheriff Wingate used his pen as a model to show any delinquent hunters as an example. The kids felt like they had won a major battle in the war on mistreated dogs but the tables would turn and Mary Beth would loose Tater, perhaps forever.

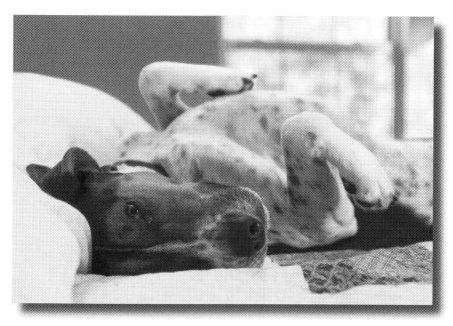

Known to be popular with English royalty, the **Beagle** and the **Southern Pointer** have a strong sense of smell and are more interested in following the scent than pleasing their owners. Deep throated barks sing together in a pack whether hunting deer or rabbits. Beagles are often used in airports to sniff out illegal food. With medium temperaments, they should be socialized around children to make good pets.

CHAPTER FIFTEEN

Alfred Snodgrass, the nosy neighbor, had been watching for signs of the Brown family going out of town. He watched from his window as the girls each took turns taking a suitcase to the car.

Linda Kaye dressed carefully the morning of the regional dog show in Raleigh. Maratee was ready and Ms. Vivian had paid the fee. Jenny and Mary Beth were both excited for their step sister and were styling their hair. Tater loped around while Maratee rolled on her back, kicking her legs in the air.

"Mary Beth, you have less than a minute to get Tater set up in the back yard." stated Ms. Vivian. Mary Beth held Tater by the collar, went out and filled the water buckets. She laid down a handful of dog biscuits and a chewy treat.

"Next year, it will be you and me, Tater." said Mary Beth to the large Dane. "We have to practice more." She hugged the dog's neck and carefully checked the gate. "Daniel will be by to feed you tonight. We will be back tomorrow night."

"Let's go!" yelled Linda Kaye, laughing. She was dressed in jeans with a white jeweled cuffs. Ms. Vivian had loaded her down with accessories (necklaces, earrings and bracelets). She knew the judges would be looking at her daughter as much as the dog. 'The girl needing to be schooled in the art of flirting and this was a fine place to start,' thought Ms. Vivian. They all loaded up it the car and pulled away leaving Tater in the back yard. Mary Beth had double checked the gate.

There was a rustling of the bushes and Mr. Snodgrass peeked through.

"There you are, you ugly mutt." Tater began barking.

"I am having a Christmas party tonight by the pool and I won't have you ruining it. Wait right there." The dog looked at him and growled. Mr. Snodgrass disappeared and reappeared at the gate holding a small piece of meat. He looking down at the cinder block pushing the gate shut and kicked it away.

"Oopsy, the little girls must be more careful, leaving you in a gate that can just swing open."

He opened the gate. Tater barked and held back. He could smell the steak in Snodgrass' hand. It was too much too resist. Tater edged up to the large man with a devilish smile and took the bait. A yellow rope with a slip knot was put over Tater's head.

"You are big as a horse, I might as well lasso you." Snodgrass laughed. He pulled the dog to the back of his mini-van where his wife was waiting. A small woman with black curly hair began barking orders at Snodgrass as soon as he appeared.

"Crawl through the back of the van and get up to the driver's seat, get out and use the window as leverage. I will push the dog in while you pull." Tater panicked and began to whimper. He was inside the van and the woman slammed the door shut.

"Drive for about an hour in any direction and dump the dog out. I will prepare the rest of the steaks for cooking. You got two hours to be back here, Alfred." And just like that, Tater was gone.

The Snodgrass party turned out to be a crowded one. There were people in the front yard and in the back yard by the pool. It was cold but Snodgrass had heated the pool and a large Christmas tree decorated the area. Colorful lights lined the fenced in yard. Cars were up and down the street and all but blocked Ms. Vivian's driveway.

The Brown family was heading home. Ms. Vivian turned the car in slowly. Maratee had gotten the blue ribbon and they all had gone out to eat in celebration. The girls were excited and Mary Beth could not wait until she could pet Tater.

Ms. Vivian, Linda and Jenny were undressing, getting into more casual attire (clothes) for the evening when they heard Mary Beth shrieking. Jenny busted out the back door and saw her sister sitting by his dog dish.

"She's gone." Mary Beth said through tears.

Jenny turned around a full three hundred and eighty degrees and could see no Tater. Then, she snapped around and walked to the open gate. Ms. Vivian and Linda Kaye joined her.

"This gate was closed proper." said Ms. Vivian is a flat tone that was full of accusation. She turned and looked at Snodgrass who was standing in this front yard. He gave her a smile and wiggled his fingers as he waved.

"Jenny, you and Linda Kaye go on foot, me and Mary Beth will go in the car and look for her.

Hopeful, at first, the girls went with enthusiasm to search for he dog but after two hours, their hearts sank with a certainty that Tater may be gone for good.

"I will put out the word at work." said Ms. Vivian. Mary Beth's tears did not cease. Ms. Vivian put the car in park and turned to her.

"Mary Beth, I see people from all over three counties and are on speaking terms with well over half of them. I know more about the people around here than a census taker. Some one will see her."

"It will be all right, Mary Beth." said Jenny, holding her sister's shoulders.

That evening, Linda Kaye put her trophy up in silence. The house which was usually filled with laughter and the sound of girl talk was silent. Ms. Vivian was on the telephone with George. She had Mary Beth go and talk to her father but it seemed to do little good.

Mary Beth sat on her bed.

"It is like when Mom did not come home from the hospital."

Jenny moved things around on her dresser but listened. Mary Beth had never talked about the accident. It was as if the air had been sucked out of the room.

"The house looks so different. I don't feel like doing my homework. I just want to sit still."

"It will be alright, Mary Beth, I promise." whispered Jennifer.

Mary Beth rubbed her legs and said, "Mom and I were going down the road. We were laughing. Mom had to slow down because it rained harder. She said, 'Mary Beth, you want to go for pizza?' That was the last thing Mom said to me ever."

Mary Beth had a blank expression. There was missing time between being in the car on the way to get pizza and the crash. The next memory was of waking up. Her leg was pinned under the glove compartment. She could not see anything but green trees and rain, grass was covering the window. They were in a ditch. She could see the fire trucks, police, highway patrol and sheriff's cars. There was an ambulance up aways. Her school project, in a large cardboard box was covering her. Her leg hurt. It felt tight, as if it were in a vice grip.

"There's another one in here!" yelled a fireman. Mary Beth told Jenny about how they asked her questions and trying to be gentle but her leg would not budge. A nurse came through her Mom's door and cleaned up the area. She sat beside Mary Beth and pulled a big sheet over there heads.

"Hi, I am Cindy. The firemen are going to pull on some metal and do some cutting, we don't want glass in our eyes." She smiled at Mary Beth. The pinch in her leg made Mary Beth scream but then there was nothing, no pain. She kept calling for her mother but no one would say a word.

Jenny hugged her sister.

"The next thing I remember is Daddy saying, 'your mama is gone. Gone up to heaven.'"

Now, Tater was gone. No one talked about Tater. Jenny now understood why Mary Beth was taking the loss so hard. All were worried but to her sister, she acted like their had been a death in the family.

The next day, Mary Beth's limp would return. There seemed to be a lot of changes in the week before Christmas break. Nick and Linda Kaye broke up. Jenny and Daniel fell back into an exclusive friendship and Katrina just waved at them in the halls. All the parents involved agreed that the kids should not hang around Uncle Cletis anymore. The club just fell apart.

Felipe came see Mary Beth. He knocked on the door and Jenny answered. He had flowers in his hand and a large Rottweiler/lab puppy on a leash.

"Come in." said Jenny. "MARY BETH, COMPANY."

"I heard about your dog. This is Sookie's puppy. He is getting big, hug." Felipe looked at his shoes and handed the flowers to Mary Beth.

"Thank you. We were just going out to hang papers for Tater with our phone number. Want to come?"

"Yeah. I would like to join the club."

"O.K. You want to help us with flyers?"

"Sure."

The kids went out in the December cold. They walked, talked and laughed. Mary Beth and Felipe hung in the back and talked.

"What did you name him?" Mary Beth asked.

"Rocky."

"I think it will be alright if you have the last of the club money to help neuter him. He may run away trying to mate and then get hit by a car if you don't." Mary Beth offered.

They papered the neighborhood, the school, Ms. Vivian's store, the pound and made copies to hand out to people in their homes. But Tater had disappeared without a trace.

CHAPTER SIXTEEN

Snodgrass had driven way out of the county and went down a road in the woods near the prison. He had to pull on Tater's rope to get her out of the van. He drove away leaving Tater along side of the road.

Tater shook. It always scared her when someone put a collar or leash on her because her life changed. She was a happy puppy with two brothers and a sister. They played all day and snuggled around their mother at night. And then, came the collar and Tater was pulled away from her mother, brothers and sister. Caged, riding in the back of a truck made Tater sick. The two little boys, Robert and Joesph, pulled her out of the cage and to the ground. They pushed their hands near her face, making her want to back away. They were rough, grabbing her and pulling her ears. She nipped one of them.

"Put that puppy in the garage. We are going to have its' ears pinned tomorrow. Did you get puppy food?" said a woman, who picked up the boy who had been nipped. Tater did not want to hurt them but her ears were long and it hurt when they were pulled.

"No. just give it whatever you give your other show dog." said a man.

Tater found herself in a dark garage without her mother and brothers and sister. There was nothing to snuggle against. She whined and cried all night long. For the first time, she learned hunger. No food was brought out to the garage that night. Only some water. Tater whined and cried for her mother.

The next day, the woman and the boys came out and opened the garage door.

"What a mess you made." said the woman.

"Ew, look, poo poo." said the boy.

They began putting their hands all around Tater and she hid in the back of the garage.

"Leave the dog alone, until it has had it's shots!" yelled the woman

The ride to the vet was just as sickening but at least there was a blanket in the cage. A woman came with a big bowl of chow and Tater wolfed it down so fast that a piece got caught in her throat. She coughed it up and kept going. Then water. She drank until her belly would bust.

The people at the vet office were nice. There were many women there with soothing voices and they all brought water and food. They cleaned up the poop and walked Tater in the grass. She loved the sunshine.

Tater hated the metal table. They stuck painful needles in her. One time she fell asleep and when she woke up, her ears hurt. She got a yucky tasting treat and the ears did not hurt as bad.

Just as she was getting to like the place, the mean lady and the mean kids came back. She was put in the car and one of the boys started putting his hands near her.

"Don't touch that dog. Having her ears pinned cost a fortune and you are not going to ruin them."

This time Tater found herself in an outdoor cage with a doghouse. The woman put a blanket in it and a bucket of water. Tater's had another dog beside her. She could tell it was a he from the smell. The dog was older but was healthy. He barked all the time and this made Tater want to bark too.

The morning routine was very quick. The man would come out and open the gate door. Tater and Barney would run around outside and "do their business". The man filled their water buckets and the woman brought out treats. She would say "Sit Sit" and Tater would sit. She would give her a dog biscuits with peanut butter.

Both dogs could hear the cars five minutes before they arrived home. Tater would start pacing. The only activity Tater enjoyed was when the woman would bring out the leash. It fit right under her chin and she would walk very fast. When Tater ran a special way, the lady would give her a treat and pet her.

Most days, she just watched the boys play and waited for food. She like the dog house. It made her feel safe. Sometimes, one of the boys would bring her table food. Sometimes good, like fatty meat, and sometimes, bad, like a banana. One day turned into the next. Tater would wake up. Pace the kennel. Bark. Eat. Watch the boys. Snuggle with her blanket. Sleep.

Tater liked the afternoon. Both dogs would listen to the cars that whisked by. Tater knew the sound of the lady's engine. She would hear it first and both dogs would get up and start pacing. With noses pressed to the gate, just seeing the lady would make Tater feel good. She wagged her tail and jumped up and down.

The lady would open the gates. "How are my babies?" Barney and Tater would bust loose around the yard and cut up for a while. The lady would grab the leashes and they would begin their walking practice down the road beside the house. The man would bring out the food. It was the best part of the day.

Tater did not like to hear the school bus. The boys would run around the yard and do their own cutting up but the taller one did not like Tater or Barney. The tall boy would kick a ball into the gate hard and sometimes threw a stick in the fence. The dogs would check it out to see if it was food and then just stare at the boys. Tater wanted to hide behind her doghouse when she saw the boys.

One day, the bus came home early. The tall boy came out to the dog kennels.

"Mom said not to go near them." said the shorter boy.

Ignoring him, the taller boy came to Barney's pen. He was wearing a jacket. Fall colors were all about and there was a nip in the air. He opened the gate. Taking a stick, he pushed Barney's bowl. There were a couple of nuggets in the bowl. Barney stiffened. He turned his head and would not look at the boy. His tail quivered. Tater began barking and jumping up and down.

"Shut up, dog" said the tall boy. He went into the pen further and kicked the bowl. Barney barked.

Tater began working her nose against the latch. She would bark and look at the boy and push the latch with her nose.

Like well stage firecrackers at the fourth of July, things were set off.

Bang. Barney lunged at the big boy and bit his arm. Pop. Tater jumped on the boy and growled at Barney. Bang. The little boy screamed. Pop. The man and the lady drove up. Bang. Tater was hit with a stick.

It was over. The man and the lady took the tall and little boy in the car. For a day Rocky nor Tater ate. The lady and the man came out the next day to feed them together. The lady was not happy. The man was angry. Tater could feel it.

"The Dane can't stay. She bit Robert."

"We don't know which one bit Robert. I have told him not to go near the dogs."

"Joesph did say Robert was in Barney's pen. How did the Dane get out?

"We agree to feed and water them and exercise them but that dog bit my kid. They gotta go."

One night things changed. The man cleaned out the kennels. It was the only time, Tater got to sniff the other dog as they were put together in one kennel while the man cleaned the other.

"Look, I don't have the money for the engine part. I done got it in my car. I will pay you some now. I got twenty."

"No, that ain't gonna work. You got something I can hold until you get your money together."

"Nothing."

"I can hold that race car of yours."

"No way. Can't we figure out something?"

"I ain't leaving here empty handed."

"My wife will kill me but what about her show dog. She's got papers."

"I want the Rottweiler."

"No, Barney is my wife's favorite, please the Great Dane. I will get the papers."

Then, Tater felt her collar go off and a rope go one. She was being pulled away.

Tater made the ride to the junk yard and became used to a diet of Tater Tots and Hot Dogs. She always got tangled in the trees. She learned thirst again. The old man would leave her all day without water.

He would untangle her but her belly was often empty and the thirst was worse than the hunger.

Then came Jenny. She loved her smell and the sight of her coming with the boy on their bicycles. She wagged her tale and danced.

The day she met Mary Beth something came over Tater. She knew this human was damaged. Tater did not know what to help but stand beside her. The girl leaned into Tater and it felt warm. Tater had not known such warmth since her mother. All living creatures want to feel the warmth of a hug.

Now, Tater found herself on a highway with many houses. Nothing smelled right. She could not smell Jenny nor Mary Beth. She sniffed for Maratee. Tater even wished she could smell Ms. Vivian's perfume, which made her sneeze. There were strange smells. Wild smells. Smells she had never known.

One day Tater smelled cats. And where there were cats, there was cat food. She found herself in the backyard of a small house. A man would bring out cat food and put it on a board. Several cats ascended on the food. When the man went inside, Tater would clean up all the food.

There was a large barn in the woods behind the house. Tater could smell food and other dogs. Digging a hole under the back door, it popped open one day.

In every cage were little dogs. They shivered in the darkness. It was cold and damp in the barn. There was only one light coming from the ceiling. Tater went from cage to cage. Some of the dogs charged the door and barked. Most were just puppies. They coughed and sneezed. Tater smelled her way around the barn. She smelled the man who fed the cat. He had been in the barn and drank beer like the man of 'the man and the lady'. A dog can tell a lot from a sniff.

There was a huge bag of dog food by the front door. Tater stood on her hind legs and knocked the bag over. With her teeth, she tore a hole in the bag. Wolfing down the food, the other dogs began to bark.

Tater began going to the cages and barking back. With her nose, Tater opened as many cage as she could. There were three Cavalier Spaniels, two Husky puppies, three Poodles and two Chocolate Labs. They all began to ear. The others barked and barked.

Tater heard the man coming.

"What can I do for you?" Tater could hear his steps. They crunched on the leaves. Metal clanged as he kicked junk aside. Then, another man spoke.

"I am Bob Wilson from Wilson's Pet Shop and I come for Lab puppies and one Husky puppy."

"Those Spaniels are not getting any younger. How about a deal, buy one get one. I need to unload them. Kennel cough. I can make you a deal on the whole lot."

"I will look at them."

As the front door opened, Tater busted out the back. One of the labs followed Tater.

"What the h..." yelled the man. He slipped and fell in the dog food.

"Wilson", he screamed. "Wilson."

"Wilson, grab these mutts before they get away."

Tater and one of the man's Chocolate Lab puppy ran through the woods, free. They did not look back. With their tales under and ears back, they were terrified.

Tater had a friend to run with through the woods but she had to look out for the puppy. Following her nose, Tater and Wilson walked onto a crowded eight lane road and the cars were really going fast. The puppy tried to cross the road and a car's horn blared at the dogs. Tater tried to pull Wilson back with her mouth but the puppy ran right in front of a mini-van which slammed on brakes. It was forced into the left lane where a car hit it. All cars came to a screeching halt. Tater looked at the people getting out of the cars, studying the damage. Some were yelling at each other. None seemed to be hurt. Wilson and Tater made their way across the interstate road.

As they were drinking from the ditch, a truck stopped.

"Wow, look at that Lab." said one man.

"The other one is huge." said the other.

Both men whistled. The man got down on one knew. He whistled, "Come on, boy." Wilson looked at Tater and the man. Wilson went to the man.

"Your going to be a great hunting dog."

They tried to get Tater but Tater only ran faster into the woods. Alone again, Tater left the highway area and went through the woods. She came upon an open field. She could smell home, feel home and through the grass, Tater ran.

Tater avoided the roads. Unaware that a car could kill her, she only wanted to avoid the strangers that tried to catch her. She knew if they got her collar, she would be trapped. Mary Beth and the back yard were on her mind. She remembered Jenny coming to give her treats. She hunted Jenny and Mary Beth like a hunting dog on a deer. Smelling the air, Tater ran to the familiar. To home.

The most popular dog with families is the **Labrador Retriever** or Lab mixes due to their soft mouths and laid back manners. Called St. John's Dogs in the early 1800s, these early labs would fetch almost anything in water, making them popular with hunters. With webbed feet, they make excellent swimmers. Easy going dogs, they make good pets.

CHAPTER SEVENTEEN

Christmas break finally arrived. It was cold but not freezing. Linda, Jenny and Mary Beth were waiting for Ms. Vivian to come home with the tree. They had been in the attic unpacking decorations for most of the morning.

"Mrs. Whitney called. She needs Cocoa washed." said Linda Kaye and she added, "She still owes us ten dollars from the last time.".

"I will call her and tell her that the club is over, but maybe will wash her dog one last time. said Jenny. She wondered if it was Cocoa, a puppy or Cocoa, the aging dog.

Mary Beth stared out the window from her wheel chair. She turned to Jenny.

"I don't believe you or Uncle Cletis. There are no animal ghost. I do not even believe in people ghost. The dogs and cats are just dead. Gone. I am glad that stupid club is over." She began to cry and rolled her wheel chair into her room.

Since the disappearance of Tater, Mary Beth went back to limping and difficulty walking. Ms Vivian refused to let her back into a wheel chair, so they argued. Mary Beth cried and sulked but Ms. Vivian would not give in. After Mary Beth fell a couple of times, Ms. Vivian allowed her to use a crutch and the chair. Loosing Tater was like losing her mother all over again. No one outside of the family cared.

Ms. Vivian pulled in with a tree so large, it was as big as the trees on the water front in the historic district. It was huge. She knew Glen, who sold the trees for the church and had finagled (managed to get) the

113

biggest one for the price of the smaller ones. Bringing the ornaments and lights from the basement, Linda Kaye and Jenny decorated the tree. Linda would stand back and go forward to rearrange the ornaments to fit her sense of style and balance. Mary Beth did not look at the tree. She stayed in her room and looked out the window.

Jenny missed the club and the friends she had made along the way. Most of all, she missed Uncle Cletis. Her greatest hope was to help her sister get over the disappearance of Tater.

"Let's go take care of Cocoa." said Linda Kaye. Jennifer got her sweater and coat and without words, they left.

The girls arrived at the large antebellum mansion around three in the afternoon and was greeting by Mrs. Whitney holding a cute German Shepard puppy.

"What's her name?" Linda Kaye fawned over the puppy and carefully took it in her arms. It licked her face and then, she petted the belly of the puppy.

"Cocoa." whispered Jenny. She looked down at the floor. Tears filled her eyes as she knew the older Cocoa was dead.

"Come into my parlor, girls. I will fix some tea. It is cold outside. As they turned the corner they saw the older Cocoa standing on crouched legs and wagging her tail.

"Cocoa!" yelled Jenny. She went over and hugged the dog, tears falling down her face.

Sitting on the couch, the girls were formally served tea on a tea tray lined with real gold. Mrs. Whitney sat down.

"Jenny, your last visit made me do some thinking. My older dog has a few more years in her but she must stay in her bed and have limited walks outside. She still eats well and goes to the bathroom on walks. The puppy tries to play and there is a little play left in my old girl. I need your club to help me with both old and new. I am getting up in years myself."

"We no longer have a club." said Linda Kaye.

"Oh, I heard all about it. As for gossip in this town, I am as well informed as your mother, Linda, but if I hear of someone that needs some help, well, let us just say my husband left me with enough money and influence to help the Henry Bergh Club of Beaufort County, Washington, North Carolina."

"Our parents' don't want us in the club anymore, Mrs. Whitney." said Jenny, with a sad expression.

"Give me their phone numbers, I have already talked to your mother Linda and she said she knows of a Henry Bergh job already!"

In the dimly lit parlor, an older woman, two girls, an old dog and a puppy had tea and cookies with the smell of dusty furniture and mothballs. A small artificial tree glimmered with Christmas lights in the corner. This was the first was several Christmas miracles to follow.

CHAPTER EIGHTEEN

The girls tore out of Mrs. Whitney' house on their bikes and headed straight to Ms. Vivian's store.

"I don't like Mary Beth left alone and I take it your homework is done." said Ms. Vivian.

"Of course, yes, mam" they spoke together with smiles as big as Ms. Vivian's dinner plate on Sunday nights.

"Been over to old lady Whitney's place, have ya?"

"Yes." giggled both girls.

"Well, wipe the grins off your faces. The county called. Your Aunt Mamie is in hot water over her cats again. I don't care about the cats but she is going to be fined this time if she has a trailer full of cats. The pound will get them day after tomorrow, Christmas Eve. Heartless. Over in Craven County there is a legal cat lady who has them fixed and they live out their life on her twelve acres. Your daddy's cousin, Chester has a camper on the back of his truck and has about twenty of those animal boxes used at the pet store. I want as many of you that you can get together and help Aunt Mamie."

"Sounds fun." said Jenny.

"It is not play. Chester is going to help all you kids, do what he says. You never handled a wild cat, girl. They ain't no purring kittens. All of you are to use leather gloves and long sleeves."

Winter was closing in on 'Little Washington' and a storm was brewing about three. It was dark and there were rumors of snow. Jenny, Linda Kaye, Nick, Katrina and Daniel heading down Belfork Road. It was dirt. A driveway make only from tire marks led up to an old single wide trailer.

"I don't have no relatives this poor." said Nick.

Katrina slapped the back of his head. His toboggan flew off.

"That's not nice, Nick." Linda Kaye frowned.

Jenny knocked on the door. You could hear the floor creak and crunch.

"Aunt Mamie, we are here for the cats."

"Come in and sit down. Chester will be here soon."

As they entered the darkened room, they all noticed it was very sparse (not many wall hangings or furniture), only one dim lamp was on in the corner of the couch. Beside an old rocker was a small pink, artifical Christmas tree with a few light. There were several kitchen chairs here and there and one old love seat.

The odor of cat urine was strong. All the kids put there noses under their coats. Then, Katrina looked up and let out a short but loud scream.

Once meant to hide curtain rods, the whole room had a long cornice, made of wood and could easily be a sitting spot for a cat. But there was not one cat, there were at least fifty cats, all staring down at the group. The cats made made warning noises, hisses and growls as the balanced themselves on the cornice. Tails twitched and curled, as the cats licked their lips.

"I am waiting outside!" yelled Katrina. Jenny came from the small bedroom.

"Guys, you have to see this! There is a mama cat having kittens.!"

All gathered round and watched the small miracle unfold. The mother was a long haired calico cat and she licked the small babies as they came out. Carefully, she took each one my it's neck and hid it in the corner. A larger kitten came from another litter. Linda picked it up and cuddled it. There was a sound coming from the yard.

Chester had arrived.

About six foot seven, Chester removed his hat and greeting Aunt Mamie with a hug. He looked like a lumberjack, tall and strong with a plaid shirt. His beard was full and covered his neck. He had bright red which was bushy and held down by his ball cap. Aunt Mamie was teary eyed.

"Now there is no for tears. We are going to be as gentle as we can be."

"They are not used to being handled, it is going to be hard on all of you."

Chester disappeared and came back with five nets. He reached up and moved the cats from the cornice with the end of pole. One fell to the floor. Chester put the net over it and scooped it up, trapping the cat which was making the worse growling noises ever heard.

"Once you bag a cat, bring the net to me, do not try to handle it. Most of these cat are feral, a few a friendly. He picked one up and it purred.

"What does "feral" mean?" asked Nick.

"When a tamed animal has gone wild, it's feral."

Gently, Linda Kaye and Jennifer put the new born kittens and the mother in a box. They took the mother over to Aunt Mamie who petted the mother cat goodbye.

So they began, in teams, each chasing cats. It was difficult getting them with nets, so Katrina, with gloves, began grabbing them by the back of the neck and dropping the cat in the net that Jenny held. Nick noticed and began catching them and delivering them to Daniel, who held the net. After about an hour, all the cats were safely in Chester's camper.

There was one cat left. The kids were hot and sweaty, they had to breath outside. Chester glanced at his watch, it was time to leave.

Daniel walked back inside and a black cat jumped at his feet and seemed to be asking for a petting.

"His name is Marvin Carter. He is a sweetie," said Aunt Mamie.

"Nice kitty." Daniel said. He reached down to pick it up and the cat hissed and scratched his face. Daniel pushed the cat away but it's right claw was stuck in Daniel's jacket.

"Help, it's caught!" screamed Daniel. He ran out to the front porch and every one looked at him like he was crazy. The cat growled and heaved back and forth trying to free itself and popped Daniel with it's claws with each failure to free itself.

Chester pulled on the cat but it was stuck but good. It attacked Daniel's face with it's claws and teeth.

"Wow, it bit my ear!" screamed Daniel.

Katrina wrapped her scarf around Daniel's face. Nick pulled on the cat and the claw went in deeper. It hissed and sprayed Daniel, as its' own territory. The odor made all cover their noses.

"Grab it from behind!" yelled Jenny.

"We can't scare it, it may sink it's claws into your friend's skull." said Chester. "Nick, I am going to put a net over Daniel and the cat, you grab it off his chest!"

Jenny could not resist. She began taking pictures of Daniel, with a scarf over his face and a net over his head with a heaving, wild cat attached to his jacket.

"I heard that!" yelled Daniel, "Stop taking pictures."

Nick readied himself for the catch, he had on thick winter gloves.

Down the net went and the cat crawled up Daniel's face and curled himself on Daniel head, like a hat from hell. It hissed and made it clear that it was vicious and would attack.

They all stood staring at Daniel who began weeping in a high pitch, later, it would be said that he "cried like a girl" but now they were concerned. It dug it's claws into Daniel's skull.

Aunt Mamie came forward and walked up the cat, softly calling "kitty, kitty" it purred and went into Ms. Mamie's arms.

"Ms. Mamie, you can keep that one cat in a carrier, as it will have to be observed for seven days, otherwise, little Daniel there will have to have a series of painful rabies shots. Who can call his mammy or pappy to take him to get a tetanus shot?"

"What is a tet-nus shot?", asked Katrina.

"It keeps you from getting the lock jaw sickness. If you step on a rusty nail or get scratched by metal, you should have one. Good for dog bites and such."

Daniel dug in his pocket and handed Jenny his cell phone.

"He'll find out sooner or later." Blinded by blood, Nick led Daniel to Ms. Mamie's shower. The water was cold. With his teeth chattering, Daniel listen to Jennifer lie to his father as she said, "he had a few scratches". Daniel had good fortune once again, like when Tater pulled him from the swamp, none of the scratches required stitching.

Seven days later, Aunt Mamie settled into her assisted living home and left Marvin Carter to feast on mice and other vermin. Occasionally, Katrina, the ever cat lover, would leave cat food near the abandoned trailer home.

CHAPTER NINETEEN

Tater walked briskly with her nose in the air. She had got a whiff of the river area and she knew that was the way to go.

Trotting on a sidewalk, Tater smelled something delightful. Food. She walked quickly toward the building, following the scent of cooked meat.

It was a shopping center only five miles away from the Brown household. There were a lot of cars in the parking lot and they carefully navigated their way around the large dog.

A Salvation Army Santa called Tater.

"Come here girl, come here."

She looked at him and smelled colon and fear. She did not like that smell. She could smell ham and turkey. It was just ahead, through the glass doors.

There was a line of people waiting for the Christmas buffet.

Tater squeezed in the door and trotted directly to the buffet

"Get the dog!"

"I think he's going to help himself."

A woman gasp as Tater put her front paws up and ate an entire pan of turkey and gravy.

Too late, the owner ran at Tater with a broom. The frightened dog jumped onto a table and had made it out the door before anyone could reach her.

The Salvation Army Santa laughed as the manager slipped while trying to hit Tater.

"Oh, shut up, Santa." said the man holding his back. Tater had once again safely crossed the road and was hugging the tree line at a fast pace. She could smell the river. She could smell the convenience store. It was like a doggie GPS in her brain. She was not lost, now the path was clear.

CHAPTER TWENTY

Finally, it was Christmas Eve. Except for Tater begin gone, Jenny was feeling happy. It had taken forever to get here and Linda Kaye was on the phone with her old friends chatting about what they wanted for Christmas. Mary Beth watched cartoons and Jenny was busy wrapping all the gifts that Ms. Vivian had bought for everyone, except her gift, of course. It was the only one Ms. Vivian had wrapped.

"I trust you not to tell anyone what their gift is, my Linda Kaye could not keep a secret if her life depended on it." Ms. Vivian said.

"Jennifer, telephone, it's Uncle Cletis!" yelled Linda Kaye.

Jennifer was a bit puzzled as she took the phone.

"Merry Christmas, Uncle Cletis!"

"I got a little something for you and your friends. Come around today if you can. You can come on Christmas or after if you are busy."

Not able to just wait, Jenny slipped off after Ms. Vivian went to work. Uncle Cletis was sitting on one of the stone benches overlooking a quiet winter garden of boxwoods. The flowers laid beneath the ground, as bulbs, waiting for spring. Uncle Cletis smoked a pipe.

Not wanting to startle him, Jenny said, "Uncle Cletis...it's me, Jennifer Brown." Without turning, Uncle Cletis answered, "I think it's going to snow." There were five gifts on the stone bench.

After sitting a minute, Uncle Cletis asked, "What is wrong?"

Jenny sighed. "It's Christmas. Tater's gone. My sister is so depressed she cries all the time. The club broke up. I miss the activity. Oh, and my Dad has to work Christmas, so does Ms. Vivian.

"Sounds like you need a small miracle." said Uncle Cletis.

"Yes, I do."

"I was thinking you would come back. I just want to ask you something. What do you see over there by that statue?"

Jenny looked up.

"That white cat. Is it yours? I see her every time I come here."

Uncle Cletis smiled. "Go pick up the cat." Jenny shrugged and walked slowly up to the animal calling, 'Kitty, kitty, kitty...'

As she reached to pick up the cat, her hands went through the cat like air and it disappeared.

"What?" Jenny looked at a smiling Uncle Cletis.

"You got the gift. I knew it when you saw Sookie. It is your destiny. You will inherit this land from me just as I inherited it from Marcus Roland." Jenny stood feeling shock and wonder.

"But there is a spirit that needs your help. You are young and are more apt to see human spirits. As you get older, you become less sensitive to the those on the other side. It is getting hard for me to see spirits."

Uncle Cletis walked over to his car and pulled out an old hat box. It looked very old. Jenny looked from behind him at the box. Inside, there was a beautiful porcelain doll.

"Up on the hill, a little girl is waiting for Christmas. She has been waiting for a hundred years for this doll. As a child, I would explore the Porter house and I have seen Adlane but she won't come to me."

Jennifer held the doll and looked at it.

"Uncle Cletis, can you tell me if Tater is dead?"

"If she is, she will show up. And I got a feeling it will be tonight. Part of the gift is that you can tell when they are coming."

"Now you wait until it warms up to go up to the Porter house. It is going to snow for sure.

Jenny took the doll and gifts. She ran home. Ms. Vivian was getting dressed for work. Hairspray and perfume could be smelled out on the porch.

The temperature dropped as the pressure off the ocean dropped and allowed the cold front from the northern states. Everyone broke out their muffs, mittens and hats to brace for freezing weather. There were rumors of hushed hopes that there would be a rare and wonderful white Christmas.

Ms. Vivian had inspected Jennifer's wrapping and placed the presents under the tree. She had talked to George and found that he would be home for New Year's but wanted the girls to go ahead and open the gifts from him on Christmas morning. Ms. Vivian poked around in the basement until she found them. The tags said they were bought long before their plans of marriage and he had bought a jewelry box for her Linda Kaye. That is why she chose George Brown from many suitors.

"Girls, I have to go. It is too cold to go out tonight, so I don't want to see you at the store." Linda hugged her Mom and said "Merry Christmas", Jenny followed suit and said "I'm sorry you have to work." Mary Beth just stared at the television.

Ms. Vivian walked over to her. Child psychology was not her strong point but she wanted Mary Beth to know she was loved, despite her behavior.

"Give me a hug, Scrooge. Stand up."

Mary Beth smiled a little and held the edge of the chair, then allowed Ms. Vivian to hold her weight as she wished her a "Merry Christmas".

Jenny looked at the clock and paced. It was only three. She looed at the hat box laying on her bed. She took out the doll and looked at it. She dreading taking the doll up there to the house but she had promised. Angry at her own fear, she lashed out and threw the doll on the bed. It looked back up to her with empty eyes.

"I'm sick of being afraid of that stupid house and I want this over with!" She looked out the window. The sun was setting. It was darker than normal. The sky was heavy with grey clouds.

After Ms. Vivian pulled her car out, Linda Kaye was on the phone and Mary Beth stared at the television petting Maratee. Jenny pulled out her gloves and a warm hat. She found the flashlight and picked up the hat box on the way out. She had a small gift for Uncle Cletis and put it in her pocket. If everything went right, she would be back home within the hour. She headed for the path off the road near the river woods, the Porter chimney loomed ahead, as if it were calling her.

CHAPTER TWENTY ONE

"Where are you going?" asked Linda.

Jenny turned around, surprised.

"I'm going for a walk, just for a while."

"It is getting dark and freezing, are you crazy?" Linda had her arms crossed and her teeth chattered.

"I am going to take Maratee for a walk. I have my cell phone and a small present for Uncle Cletis in this bag. I will go by his house and put it inside the door. I will be back in an hour tops." Maratee appeared with her leash and went out alongside Jenny . Inside bag was the doll and a small present of after shave lotion. She carried a flashlight in the other hand turned briefly to wave goodbye.

With that Jenny was gone.

"Whatever." said Linda Kaye. She looked at the angel on top of the tree and yelled, "but be careful!"

It was not nearly as hard to navigate through the thicket as the foliage had died off for the winter. Still, there were evergreens thick and full. Jenny shined the flashlight on the ground and then up to the path and back on the ground. Through years of exploration, the Porter path was well worn and easy to see. It was just after five but that was nearly dark in the winter.

The house appeared a dark sky. The moon peaked out from behind the clouds which were heavy with snow. Jenny steadily walked toward the house, breathing a little hard from walking in the cold. She could hear noises behind her and did her best to fight her imagination. Maratee enjoyed being out and leaped over the small branches in her way.

Entering the door of the house, Jenny felt a little dizzy, closed her eyes and held her head. Opening her eyes, Jenny was astonished to see the house was as new as the day it was built for a few seconds. Then, it morphed into the old run down house of today Forcing her legs to move, she walk to where there was a stairway and saw a little girl with blonde hair. Adlane was there, laughing in her white sleeping gown. Passing right through Jenny, she walked to the tree. It was decorated with a string of popcorn and silver ornaments. A small boy appeared and looked under the tree with Adlane. Laughing, he picked up a match and lit a small candle on the tree. Just as before, Adlane lit the candles one by one.

Seconds later, the tree was on fire. The boy ran up the stairs to wake his parents but began choking and fell on a step. Adlane ran out of the house in the woods. Jenny followed her with the bag in her hand.

"I am here." said Adlane from the woods.

"Adlane, Adlane! Stop! I have your doll!" yelled Jenny. She could see the child's white gown dash in-between trees. Maratee could see better than Jenny. Jenny ran into the tall vines that covered both ground and limbs from the above. Pointy thorns tore at her jeans. Maratee yelped. Jenny fell. Her cell phone fell out of her pocket. Covered with dirt and scratches, she stood up and decided that she could not continue. Night had fell in and Jenny had gotten turned around. She was lost on Christmas Eve in the woods. Shaking her head at her own stupidity, she started to turn back and then saw Adlane ahead.

It was freezing cold and snow flakes began falling from the sky as dainty dancers in free form ballet. Jennifer looked up and really saw the big, white, fluffy flakes come down. Why was she not enjoying the snow from the safety of her own bed? Jenny wished she had stayed home. Turning and walking a few more feet, she hesitated, feeling afraid, and then a few more feet. Jenny walked in a clearing away from the trees and suddenly, the earth fell from her feet. She dropped in a hole and grabbed what felt like a muddy root. At he same time she heard the loud voice of a young girl.

"I AM HERE!"

Crying out, Jenny knew she was in real trouble. She held the bag and flashlight in one hand and the branch in the other. She let the bag drop, not caring about the doll or Uncle Cletis' present anymore. She heard it hit water within a few seconds. The flashlight revealed that she was in an old well. The stones that made the circular walls were mud covered and thick with vines. Shining the flashlight down, Jenny felt pure panic. If she fell, the fall would kill her. Shining the light up, the root looked big, she would need both hands to pull herself up, if the root held. Gasping, she had to drop the flashlight, to get a better grasp.

"Help!" she screamed. She could hear nothing, lost in the woods, it was most likely no one could hear her cry for help. Maratee barked and barked. Maybe someone would hear the shrill yaps.

And then, Jenny heard the voice of an angel. "I am here, too."

Jenny looked up to she her mother sitting on the edge of the well like she was sitting, reading a bedtime story.

"Hold on, there is a stronger root just above your left hand, you are going to have to push your fingers in the mud to find it." To Jenny's amazement, it was there and it was strong.

"Lift your dangling left foot up and you will feel a brick. You can put your weight on it. Hold on sweetie, help is on the way." Jenny complied and found the brick. A sense of calmness came over her.

"Mom." She looked up and Maratee continued to yap.

All she saw was darkness and snow falling like kisses from the sky.

CHAPTER TWENTY TWO

Linda Kaye woke up Mary Beth. It was nearly midnight.

"Jenny never came home and I can't get her on her cell."

Mary Beth lifted herself up and examined Jenny's empty bed. Both girls looked out the window.

"Snow!" Exciting, both girls went to the window and watched the snow come down before an area light. The snow was big and fluffy, the kind that would "stick", as George would say. Mary Beth had never seen snow and Linda had only seen it once when she was four.

"We have to find Jenny before Mom comes home, she gets off at two."

Networking on her phone, Linda Kaye had Daniel, Katrina and even, Nick heading toward the Brown house. Each was more than willing to climb out their windows, just to experience snow. It was cold but the snow actually absorbs the dampness in the air, so it was a dry cold.

With Katrina on one side and Linda on the other, Mary Beth placed her arms around their necks and walked to the road. She actually was walking more on her own than she knew but the shoulders of friends gave her the strength to move.

"Let's go to my Uncle's house first." said Katrina. It would take a good fifteen minutes just to get there.

There were not too many cars on the road. Most of the stores had shut down early for the Christmas holiday. Ms. Vivian worked in one of the few stores that kept regular hours.

"We'll make a killing." said Ms. Vivian's boss to her three days prior until Christmas.

"No, you will make a killing. Working until two is killing me. Find yourself another fool." said Ms. Vivian.

"I will give you two more dollars an hour." said her boss in a chiming tone.

"You will double my salary on holidays and provide Christmas dinner." said Ms. Vivian. The little man reluctantly agreed. It would turn out to be very busy and he needed experience behind the counter. Ms. Vivian was content to ring up the last minute stocking stuffers with the thought of her children sleeping soundly in bed.

George's plans had changed. His boss decided to let him off and he would be home tomorrow and they would have a wonderful Christmas day. Unknowing to George his daughter was in danger and an informal search party had begun looking for her.

"Now, remember, I warned you about Uncle Cletis. No one has ever seen these dog ghost and cat spooks but him. I just hope Jenny is there." said Katrina. "So, if any of you tell anyone about this little crazy trip we are having, I will be busting some ..."

"Katrina, it's our secret. Besides, being with all of you is the coolest thing I have ever done." stated Daniel

Ten minutes seemed like an hour but they finally made it to Uncle Cletis' house which was made of cinderblock covered with vinyl siding. A dim light on the porch barely illuminated the door. The trees were overgrown and it was spooky at night. Katrina knocked on the door. She put her ear to the door and heard shuffling. This embarrassed Katrina but she was committed now. No turning back.

"Who is it? I got my baseball bat." yelled Uncle Cletis from the inside.

"It's me. Katrina." yelled the young girl.

"Who?"

"Katrina. Your sister, Dee Dee's girl." The door creaked open slightly.

"Is Jenny here? She is missing!" yelled Katrina. This woke Uncle Cletis up. He opened the door all the way revealing the rag tag gang on his porch, with the snow they looked like something out of a Dickens novel.

"Oh my goodness, this is my fault. I told her to take a doll up to the Porter place but I thought she would do it during daylight." All the kids gathered inside, snow and moisture on their jackets. Uncle Cletis gathered his coat and hat.

"I don't know, I said something about the spirits... maybe she went up to my graveyard." He shook his head as he went out to his car. He felt like an old fool. How could he have misguided Jenny in that way?

"I told y'all he's crazy. Don't be blaming me if we end up lost." said Katrina.

Mary Beth looked at her.

"I hope we find my sister. I can't lose anyone else. First Mom, then our dad goes away, then Tater. Please, I don't want anything for Christmas but my sister back."

Cletis stomped the gas a few times and the engine fired right up. It was loud and knocked a bit. The kids began talking and Cletis considered the best plan of action.

"I will drop you boys at the path of the Porter house. I have flash lights. Check it and call if you find anything. We will trace her path to my cemetery and she if she is there, you boys come meet us there."

They pulled up to the old dirt road. Cletis got out and unlocked the gate. They continued to the woods beyond and the full moon was hanging large in the sky. It was silhouetted with trees and clouds and with the snow, it was a remarkable sight to see. Snow was sticking to the ground.

Cletis helped Mary Beth out. All of them walked around with their hands in their pockets waiting.

Katrina leaned against the car. She just shook her head. Suddenly, she heard a meow. She jumped. A long hair gray cat sat on the roof of the car and just stared at Katrina.

"This old gray cat nearly scared me to death." she said while she laughed.

"What old gray cat?" asked Linda Kaye.

"He is right..." Katrina turned and the cat was gone.

"It must of run off."

"That was your Grandma Reddy's cat." said Cletis.

"It was not a ghost cat, it was a real cat." argued Katrina.

Oh!" She screamed. It was at her feet.

Mary Beth said, "I see it. Here kitty, kitty, kitty."

"I still don't see it." said Linda Kaye.

The boys came running up the hill.

"No sign of her." said Nick, out of breath. Both boys froze. Their eyes opened wide in disbelief. All the kids felt wonder and amazement. Hundreds of transparent dogs and cats were all milling around. Some cats were in the trees, hissing at the dogs below. There were a few horses. Dogs sniffed and wagged their tails. A few puppies ran toward Mary Beth and she went to pick them up and they disappeared. Some of the animals were solid but some you could see right through.

"It's real, it's true. You are not a lunatic, like my daddy says you are." said Katrina. Scared she went to hug her uncle's neck.

"They won't hurt you. Now, at least, you know I am not crazy."

The kids stared in wonder as cats and dogs mingled around their feet.

"I can't see them much, but I can hear them better." said Mary Beth.

Uncle Cletis said, "I am glad all of you know but I do not see Jenny. I think we need to drive over to sheriff's house and, heaven help us all, over to the store and tell Ms. Vivian."

The animals began fading into the ground, the sky and into the woods.

"Where are they going?" asked Daniel.

"Back into the realm between life and death, they will be there until someone loves them enough to treat them with care and kindness. Then the animal's spirit will bond with a human host spirit and never have to return to earth again. A lab wagged it's tail and begged Uncle Cletis for a pet.

Snow had begun to accumulate on the ground and there was about four inches, a major event for Washington, North Carolina. A true white Christmas.

Mary Beth cried. Linda Kaye held her. Nick held Linda's hand. Daniel and Katrina just looked forward. And then Mary Beth stopped crying. She opened the car door and got out on her feet, fell and got up again, pointing.

"Jenny!" yelled Mary Beth.

"Where?" yelled Linda.

Then they all turned to see two silhouetted figures coming toward them with the moon shining on their features. It was Jenny and with her was a large Great Dane. It was Tater. All ran and hugged Jenny and

Tater who licked Mary Beth's face without mercy. Maratee pranced along-side of them.

"What happened?" were the words on everyone's lips.

Jenny began to speak, excited, she almost lost her breath.

"I had gone to the Porter house. I am sorry, I should have gone in the day but I wanted to get this out of the way. But anyways, I made it up by the path. The house seemed to come alive and I saw Adlane and a little boy. Adlane lit a candle that started the fire and she ran out of the house. I chased her and fell into a well."

Everyone hung on Jenny every word, they barely noticed the occasional animal spirit that walked near the group.

"I thought I would fall to my death. I grabbed a root and as I put my weight on it, it felt as if it would snap. I got a foot hold and reached up. I got one hand on the ground. Then, I heard Tater barking."

Mary Beth hugged Tater even tighter. He was not a spirit but very alive. Very alive and muddy.

"Maratee barked and barked. Tater must of heard her. I slipped back into the well. The branch gave way and I fell a few more feet. Luckily, there was a piece of board jutting out from the well wall and I hung on. All I could hear was Tater's barking.

Then, I heard men talking. A flash light shined on me and I yelled, "help". It Felipe and his father! Felipe ran back and got a rope while his father held on to me. I did not know it, but I was nearly out of the Porter woods. One of the old trailer parks was right there and Tater's bark woke them up. Filipe pulled me up. They wanted to bring me home but I convinced them that I would be in big time trouble and I could find my way home."

"I wish we could ask where Tater has been?" said Mary Beth.

They all petted the dog. Tater went stiff and barked. The large dog stood and wagged her tail but stared intently.

Jenny hugged Uncle Cletis and whispered in his ear, "I saw her. I saw Mom. I have the gift." Uncle Cletis smiled and shook his head 'yes' and hugged her even tighter. It felt like Christmas.

The group looked in the distance following Tater's stare and saw the unbelievable. Adlane stood with her dolly. She smiled. "I just wanted my

Christmas present." The ghost girl began dancing with the animal ghost and they all were drawn to her. As she disappeared into the unknown realm, they followed.

"Look, the pets are going to heaven with her." said Daniel. They all jumped in Uncle Cletis' car and no one spoke.

Scurrying, Uncle Cletis pushed the gas petal to the floor. He had to beat Santa. First, he dropped Nick off at his home, where he slipped back into his bedroom. Then, went Daniel, who had to tip toe into the shower and put his pajamas back on. Stopping at the Brown household was lucky, as they only beat Ms. Vivian by a few minutes.

On the way back to her family's neighborhood, Katrina said, "Uncle Cletis, I am so proud that you are my uncle. All my life, people say, Uncle Cletis is crazy or Uncle Cletis drinks or some mess. I want to help you out with the pets as much as you need me." Uncle Cletis smiled. He had gotten his Christmas wish.

Christmas morning came. Tired the girls opened their presents, happy to have each other, no gift could come close to bringing that amount of joy they had felt in the boneyard, except for one. Ms. Vivian had taken a picture of the Henry Bergh Club when they first started out. It was framed and Jenny smiled. Mary Beth opened a large gift wrapped in green and blue paper with snowflakes. Inside was a dog vest, bright red. It said Therapy Dog on the side. Tater and Maratee just watched, wagging their tales.

"Tater!" The dog walked over her and allowed her to put the vest on. You are a therapy dog, not a show dog."

The rest of the school year went by fast. Linda Kaye had given up her entourage of admirers and socialized with her real friends, the ever growing members of the Henry Bergh Club. Each member took some grief from their peer groups but it passed as sure as the seasons did. Winter turned to spring and summer ended another school year. Daniel and Jenny's secret swimming pond had been closed off with a new housing development as expected.

Another year later, Jenny would go to the police and tell them about falling into a well on a childish venture to give a doll to a ghostly girl. A deputy took an interest and found the well while off duty. With equipment, the bones of a young female were retrieved. Adlane's funeral was an event. The whole town came and it made headlines even in the state newspaper.

Mary Beth never had trouble walking again. She began practiced with Tater along with Linda Kaye and Maratee but soon realized that Tater was her therapy dog. With Tater by her side, her confidence grew. A psychologist certified Tater to wear a vest and Mary Beth graduated high school with Tater at her side

Occasionally, the founding members of the Henry Bergh Club members would successfully go and see the animal spirits at night but as time passed, only Jenny could see them as she grew older. George and Ms. Vivian would remain together as husband and wife. She finally was able to quit her convenience store job as George was promoted and the family moved closer to his job.

Bergh founded the ASPCA for the horse, mankind survived the caves and hunted game with the dog, but for some, the cat is the "purrfect" pet. If you do not have the time to exercise with a dog, cats are excellent for therapy animals. Found in murals of ancient Egypt, cats have helped man control rats and snakes for thousands of years. Children should be careful with cats as they have retractable claws. While not eager to please humans, for some humans, cats are the most pleasing.

EPILOGE

Linda Kaye and Jenny graduated from high school together. George and Ms. Vivian sat in the auditorium, applauding for each daughter as they received their diplomas. School had given them the essential skills needed to live but both girls had been equally influenced during the summer of Uncle Cletis, ghost stories and the Henry Bergh Club.

Linda Kaye participated in land conservation classes. Loving to work with plants, she landed a job at a greenhouse. This job allowed her to save money for her own landscaping company. Linda Kaye Yarkworks became known throughout eastern North Carolina.

Mary Beth went to the local community college and later transferred to a college where she could follow her dream of becoming a child therapist. She opened an office in Raleigh, the state capitol, and was known to be believer in pet therapy for troubled youths. Even though Tater was gone, Mary Beth would always have a dog, one from the local shelter.

Katrina married a year after high school. Her husband was in the military and while being stationed in Germany, Katrina worked for a dog groomer. Eventually returning home, Katrina opened a grooming business which financed a facility for homeless cats.

Daniel went to college and majored in journalism. He won an award with a story called The Henry Bergh Club. After being hired at a newspaper two hours away from Washington, he petitioned for having a page devoted to animal shelter dogs and cats. He was responsible for the feature story each year.

Nick and Jenny both went to Beaufort County Community College for law enforcement. Graduating, Nick became an animal welfare officer. Jenny worked in the 911 center until her twenty-first birthday. Everyone was mystified as to why she would take a county job with the local animal shelter for less money but she did. Uncle Cletis died a year later and she inherited the grounds past the landfill. Close to fifty acres, Jenny would not entertain any offer from developers.

But most of all, to everyone's dismay, Jenny insisted on working at the hill. Felipe worked with her. Although his family moved on, he remained in Washington. Jenny would often sit and talk to the white cat. Her gift was strong. Jenny knew she was the keeper of that gate which connected this world and the next and she had the white cat to keep her company.

Printed in the United States
By Bookmasters